Feeling steamy . . .

"Just calm down, okay?" a woman's voice responded, sounding much calmer. "Let's talk about this like adults."

"Hey, isn't that Tessa?" Bess whispered, her blue eyes wide.

I nodded, easily recognizing the spa owner's melodious voice. I also recognized the anger in her companion's voice, and it worried me. When people sound like that, it usually means trouble. Concerned for Tessa, I leaned forward so I could hear better. But I shouldn't have bothered. The unknown man's voice burst out again, loud enough to make us all jump a little.

"I'm done trying to talk to you, Tessa!" he shouted furiously. "And mark my words. By the time I get through with you, you won't be able to shut down this stupid place fast enough!"

NANCY DREW
girl detective™

Available from Simon & Schuster

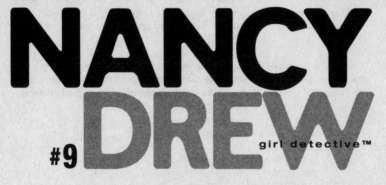

NANCY DREW

girl detective™

#9

Secret of the Spa

CAROLYN KEENE

Aladdin Paperbacks
New York   London   Toronto   Sydney

First Aladdin Paperbacks edition January 2005

Copyright © 2005 by Simon & Schuster, Inc.

ALADDIN PAPERBACKS
An imprint of Simon & Schuster Children's Publishing Division
1230 Avenue of the Americas, New York, NY 10020

Manufactured in the United States of America
10   9

NANCY DREW is a registered trademark of
Simon & Schuster, Inc.

ALADDIN PAPERBACKS, NANCY DREW: GIRL DETECTIVE, and colophon
are trademarks of Simon & Schuster, Inc.

Library of Congress Control Number 2004106074

ISBN-13: 978-0-689-86858-0   ISBN-10: 0-689-86858-8

Contents

Talk of the Town

Nancy? Nancy? Earth to Nancy Drew!"

I blinked, snapping out of a daydream as I picked at some lint in my bedroom carpet. "Sorry, Bess," I said, swallowing a yawn. "What were you saying?"

Bess Marvin, one of my best friends, dipped her nail polish wand into the bottle of pink liquid on the desk in front of her and studied me. She propped one bare foot on the edge of my desk.

"Weren't you listening to what I just said, Nancy?" she demanded.

My other best friend, George Fayne, smirked and rolled over on my bed. "Poor Nancy had probably passed out from the nail polish fumes." George waved one hand in front of her face and wrinkled her nose.

Bess rolled her eyes. Even though she and George are cousins, they couldn't be more different. If Bess is everyone's idea of the perfect girl, with her blond hair and pretty, feminine dresses, George defines the word *tomboy*. She keeps her dark hair cropped short—wash-'n'-wear hair, as she calls it—and lives in jeans and sneakers.

I fall somewhere in the middle of the two of them. I'm nowhere near as interested in clothes and makeup as Bess—I'm lucky if I remember to dab on a little lip gloss most days. And I occasionally might even forget to comb my hair before leaving the house. On the other hand I don't mind doing a little shopping now and then, or putting on a pretty skirt and some makeup for a special date with my boyfriend, Ned.

Somehow, though, despite all our differences, our three-way friendship works. George and I do our best to tolerate Bess's incurable love of clothes, Bess and I try to look interested when George starts rambling on about the latest computer gadget she wants to buy, and the two of them are always ready to help out with my own favorite hobby—solving mysteries. Lucky thing, too, since that's something I've loved doing since I was knee high to a leprechaun, as my father would say. I've never really gone around looking for puzzles to figure out and crimes to solve. They just seem to find me.

At the moment, however, without a case to solve, I felt a little bored. I usually enjoy just hanging out in my room with my friends, but I was feeling kind of restless. "I was just saying that I wonder how much it would cost to have this done at Indulgences." Bess gestured toward her pink toenails.

George groaned dramatically. "Do you *have* to keep bringing up that stupid place every two seconds?" she asked.

I glanced at her in surprise. Bess had been talking almost nonstop about the fancy new day spa scheduled to open that weekend in our hometown of River Heights. It was a little annoying, true—but George sounded downright irritated. That wasn't really like her. She can be impatient, but she usually finds Bess's girlier interests and comments more amusing than annoying.

Bess didn't seem to notice George's reaction. She was staring into space thoughtfully, the nail polish wand suspended over her foot. "Do you think it's going to be as expensive as everyone says?" she mused. "I mean, they don't actually mention any prices in the commercials or anything. But I heard the price for a facial is going to be three times as much as it would be at Head to Toe."

"I guess they have to pay their expenses somehow," I commented, sitting up and leaning against the foot of my bed. "They rebuilt the old candy factory practically from scratch. And that fancy Roman bath–style mud room thing they show on the ads doesn't look like it was cheap to build either."

Bess nodded. "That looks cool, doesn't it?" she said. "I heard the owner, Tessa What's-her-name, designed it herself. I guess it's supposed to be the centerpiece of the whole place. The article about the grand opening in this morning's newspaper says they imported something like seventy-five different types of mud from all over Europe and South America, and the tiles in the mud room were all handcrafted in Spain. I've never seen anything like that around here."

I nodded. From what I could tell from the television commercials that had been running almost nonstop for the past couple of months, none of us had seen anything like Indulgences before—at least not in our quiet Midwestern town. River Heights features numerous barber shops and a handful of salons, including one called Head to Toe that offers a few spa services such as facials and massages. But Indulgences was going to be different—the kind of fancy, full-service spa one might find in a big city like Chicago or New York. It was supposed to feature everything needed for a day of relaxation and rejuvenation, including mud baths and saunas, a staff of masseuses, a lap pool, and even a restaurant and juice bar.

"I bet it'll be successful," I said. "River Heights might not be a very big city, but there are lots of wealthy people here, partly because of Rackham Industries. I'm sure a lot of people would like to get pampered in style now and then, even if it costs a little more than they're used to."

Bess nodded. "I hear that," she said. "In fact, I was just thinking it might be fun to go to the grand opening tomorrow and splurge on a facial or something." She grinned, revealing the dimples in her cheeks. "Maybe we could even check out that Roman mud bath!"

"Forget it!" George growled, her voice suddenly so loud that I jumped a little. "There's no way I'm wasting my time on something like that."

Bess scowled at her. "Fine! You don't have to bite my head off, though," she said, sounding slightly wounded. "It was just an idea."

I stared at George, startled by her hostility. As I said, she's usually much more tolerant of Bess's interests even when she doesn't share them. Why would she get upset about something so minor? I wondered if she was having money trouble again. George isn't what you could call a master budgeter. Usually any money she earns is spent the second she gets it, if not

5

before. And she can be a little touchy when she's feeling broke.

Even George herself seemed to realize her reaction was a little over the top. "Sorry," she muttered, not meeting our gaze. "I just wish we could talk about something other than that stupid spa for a change, that's all."

"Have I been talking about it that much?" Bess said sheepishly. "Sorry. Hey, but that reminds me—I meant to ask you guys if you saw that new show on TV last night. . . ."

We were still chatting when there was a knock on the half-open door a few minutes later. I glanced over and saw my father standing in the doorway. He poked his head in and looked around, taking in the scene—Bess with one foot still propped on the desk, half her toenails painted pink; George lounging on the bed picking her teeth; and me sprawled lazily on the floor. He smiled.

"Sorry to interrupt," he said. "It looks like you girls are in the middle of some very important business."

"Very funny, Mr. Drew!" Bess said, smirking.

There aren't many people in River Heights who would dare joke around with Carson Drew. He's one of the toughest, most highly respected, and successful lawyers in town. But Bess and George have known my father since they were in diapers, so they see right through his big reputation to the sweet, funny, caring man he is, outside the office and the courtroom.

Sometimes I wonder what my family might have been like if my mother hadn't died when I was three. But one thing I can't imagine is not being as close to Dad as I am, thanks to so many years of relying on him to be both father and mother to me. It's also tough to picture not having Hannah Gruen in our lives—she's been our housekeeper practically forever and is totally a part of the family.

Dad stepped into the room. "Hey, you girls had better be nice to me," he teased, his eyes twinkling. "Otherwise I might not share the exciting free gift I just received and came up here to tell you about."

"What is it?" George immediately sounded interested. She always loves getting stuff for free.

Dad reached into his pocket. "I just finished a case for Ms. Tessa Monroe, owner of Indulgences Spa," he said. "I guess she appreciated my efforts, because she gave me these free passes for her grand opening tomorrow." He pulled his hand out of his pocket to reveal several tickets. Then he shrugged and grinned. "Now, I don't think a facial is really going to do much for my old mug, and I've got an unnatural fear of saunas. So I started thinking, who do I know who might be able to use such a thing?"

"Me! Us!" Bess squealed, leaping up out of her chair so fast that she almost upended her nail polish all over my desk. She grabbed it just in time, righted it, then rushed over to grab the tickets out of Dad's hand, as if fearing he might take them away. "Oh, thank you, Mr. D! We were just talking about how awesome it would be to go, and how expensive it is. . . ."

Dad laughed at her enthusiasm. "You're welcome," he said. "But if you girls are going to use the passes, you'll have to break the news to Hannah and her bridge club. They were next on the list."

"Oh. Do you think Hannah wants one of the passes?" Bess asked immediately, a look of concern crossing her pretty face.

I chuckled. Hannah is what some people might call "a handsome woman." From what I can tell, that means she's attractive in a no-nonsense, practical, get-away-from-me-with-that-perfume-sample-if-you-value-your-kneecaps kind of way. She never fusses much over her clothes or her short, salt-and-pepper hair. I could easily imagine her enjoying a free day at the theater or a gardening expo or even the zoo. But a fancy day spa? No way.

"I think Hannah will be okay," I assured Bess. Then I shot my father a smile and wink. "Thanks, Dad."

"No problem." Dad glanced at his watch. "Gotta go. I need to make a couple more calls before dinner.

Hannah says it'll be ready in half an hour, by the way."

"Okay."

He hurried off down the hall. I glanced at Bess, who was staring gleefully at the passes in her hand.

"I guess your dream came true, Bess," I teased playfully. "Looks like we're spa-ing it up tomorrow."

"Yeah," George said, her voice flat. "Looks that way."

Bess shot her a glance. "Oh, come on," she said. "It's not like you'll have to spend a cent of your hard-earned money. You can't possibly complain about going now."

"Want to bet?" George muttered.

I shot her a curious glance. "Don't you think it could be fun?" I asked, honestly perplexed that she was still dragging her feet now that the money issue was solved. "I mean, I'm not exactly a spa buff either, but it will be cool to check out the new place and get a little pampering, right?"

George just shrugged. Her face was still set in a frown.

Bess and I exchanged a glance. It was no surprise that a day of facials and manicures wasn't making George jump for joy, but normally she was up for trying something new and different—especially something free.

"Are you okay?" Bess asked her cousin with concern.

9

"Of course!" George responded quickly. "Why do you ask?"

"It's just that you seem so down on this whole spa thing—"

"Fine, fine," George interrupted grudgingly. "If it means that much to you to go let someone rub mud all over you and stuff, I guess I'll give it a try. It might not be that horrible."

I grinned at Bess. "That's the spirit!" we said in unison.

When we trooped downstairs a few minutes later, we found Hannah in the kitchen. She was humming softly under her breath as she mixed something in a large ceramic bowl. There was a large pot bubbling on the stove nearby, and the enticing scent of her special seafood chowder filled the room, making my mouth water. The small television on the counter was tuned to a local news broadcast, the sound turned down low.

"Smells great, Hannah," I said hungrily, taking a deep sniff.

Hannah glanced up and smiled at me. "Should be ready before long."

"Hey, you guys!" Bess said urgently, staring at the TV set. She hurried over and turned up the volume. "Check it out—they're talking about Indulgences!"

George rolled her eyes. "For a change," she muttered sarcastically.

I stepped forward to peer at the tiny screen. "Isn't that Marletta Michaels?" I asked, recognizing the reporter, a striking woman in her fifties with an impressive upsweep of platinum blond hair. "I thought she usually covered, like, real news stories." I shot Bess an apologetic glance. "You know what I mean."

"You're right, Nance," George said. "But she's also a real supporter of vegetarianism, remember?"

I nodded, recalling a two-part series the reporter had done recently about the health benefits of a vegetarian diet. "I remember. So what?"

"Nancy, haven't you been paying any attention at all?" Bess puffed out a loud sigh, sending a strand of her blond hair flying. "Honestly, I don't know how you can be so sharp and organized about solving mysteries and so scatterbrained about everything else . . ."

I just grinned. It wasn't the first time I'd heard that. Bess's exasperated comment was just a variation on what my friends, my father, Hannah, and/or Ned told me every time I accidentally left the house wearing mismatched socks or locked my car keys in the trunk for the umpteenth time.

"So fill me in," I said. "What's the connection here?"

"Indulgences is supposed to be totally vegetarian

and organic and stuff," Bess explained. "It's one of their big selling points. I'm sure that's why Marletta Michaels is interested in it."

Sure enough, when we stopped talking long enough to listen to what the reporter was saying, I realized she was discussing the spa's organic vegetarian menu. ". . . and absolutely no meat *at all,*" Marletta finished, sounding very pleased as she emphasized the last two words. "A breath of fresh air in this area, indeed. I know I'll be first in line to sample their secret-recipe vegetarian chili." She smiled at the camera. "And now, over to Stacey Kane with a look at how the grand opening will affect another local business."

The picture switched to a different reporter, this one a pretty young blond woman. She was standing on the sidewalk in front of the Head to Toe salon.

"Guess they're trying to find out how the competition feels about the new place," George commented.

The young reporter started interviewing the proprietors of Head to Toe, a pair of grandmotherly looking women wearing matching pink aprons over their neat pantsuits. While the reporter maintained a concerned expression, the two older women never stopped smiling pleasantly.

Hannah glanced up from her cooking. "It's a

shame," she commented. "Those ladies over at Head to Toe have really built up a nice business for themselves over the years. Hope this new place doesn't steal too many of their customers away."

"It probably will," George said darkly. "A big, fancy place like this new spa could run them right out of business."

I shrugged. "I doubt it," I said, turning away from the TV as a commercial came on. "They don't seem to be going after the same kind of clientele, you know? Head to Toe isn't really a full-service spa or anything. It's just a place where people can get a little extra pampering while they get their hair cut."

"I think Nancy's right," Bess agreed. "Indulgences seems more like it's trying to appeal to the country club set. People like that don't go to Head to Toe for haircuts and facials anyway—they probably travel to a bigger city or something."

"Maybe you're right." George leaned against the kitchen counter. "But I'd hate to think we helped send those nice ladies out of business, you know? Maybe we should spend the day at Head to Toe tomorrow instead. You know, support local small business."

I stared at her. "What is *up* with you today?" I demanded, my curiosity finally taking over. "Why are you so down on Indulgences? It's like you have a personal vendetta against it. Did Tessa Monroe once knock you down and steal your ice-cream cone or something?"

George refused to meet my gaze. Instead she stared fixedly at Hannah's mixing bowl. "That reminds me, it's almost dinnertime," she said. "If I'm going to have to spend all day tomorrow in vegetarian land, I'd better fill up tonight."

Without another word she hurried out of the kitchen. We could hear her sneakers slapping against the hallway floor, then the sound of the front door swinging open and quickly slamming shut.

"What was that all about?" I wondered aloud. "Is it just me, or was she acting really strange?"

Bess shrugged. "You got me," she said, already heading toward the door. "But we'll have to discuss it later. George drove me here. See you tomorrow!"

She took off at top speed. I wandered out of the kitchen and into the next room, where I watched from the window as Bess caught up with her cousin just in time to stop her from driving off without her. A second after Bess climbed in, George's car took off with a squeal of tires.

I watched it go, still astonished at George's behavior. What in the world was wrong with her?

The Grand Opening

W ow," Bess commented. **"Looks** like we weren't the only ones who were curious about this place."

It was Saturday morning, and my friends and I had just climbed out of my car, which I'd parked at a meter about three blocks down from Indulgences. We'd cruised past the spa, looking for a closer spot, but both sides of the street were jam-packed with cars. Someone had even parked a large SUV across the delivery entrance to a fancy Italian restaurant a few doors down from the spa, and an officer from the River Heights police was standing beside it writing out a ticket, while an exasperated-looking man in a chef's hat and apron waved his arms around nearby.

"You're not kidding," I told Bess, stepping back out of the way as a pair of chattering, excited, middle-aged ladies made a beeline for the growing queue at the spa's entrance. "I hope the rest of the businesses around here weren't counting on getting any customers today."

I glanced up and down the street as we neared the spa. Indulgences was located in one of the now nicer shopping districts in town, which consisted of several tree-lined blocks packed with restaurants and boutiques. The spa was sandwiched between an expensive dress shop and a small park. A high-end pet store called the Pampered Pooch was right across the street, with clothing boutiques on either side of it. Shopkeepers and clerks were standing in the doorways of several of the shops, watching the commotion in front of Indulgences.

Bess shrugged. "I don't know," she said. "Maybe they'll actually get more business. The spa is certainly attracting a lot of people to the area—some of them are bound to do a little shopping while they're here, right?"

"Enough with the marketing talk," George said. "I thought this was supposed to be a day of relaxation."

Bess and I chuckled and agreed. I had already noted that George sounded slightly more cheerful than she had the day before. She'd even dressed up a little for the occasion, putting on a pair of funky sunglasses and one of Bess's stylish hats. She was probably just in a bad mood yesterday. Happens to the best of us—no biggie.

As we reached the front of the spa I took in the scene. The building itself had undergone a lot of construction since it had first been built, and was now a clean, modern structure that somehow fit in perfectly with the older, more traditional structures surrounding it. The stucco exterior was painted a serene shade of greenish beige, with subtle rust-colored accents. It was set back from the street a little, leaving space for a small Japanese-style rock garden and a teak path leading to the front entrance. The lobby of the spa was fully visible from the street through wide glass windows that reached from floor to ceiling.

"Wow," Bess said. "It looks even nicer in real life than it did on TV!"

I didn't answer for a moment, distracted by a flurry of activity over near the front of the line at the entrance. Glancing in that direction, I spotted a familiar face. "Hey, look over there," I told my friends. "It's Marletta Michaels."

Bess and George followed my gaze toward the TV reporter. Marletta was standing a few yards away from the line of customers waiting to get inside. She was holding a microphone under one arm as she peered intently into a hand-held mirror and fluffed up her blond hair, which seemed to be piled even higher on her head than usual. A burly cameraman stood a few feet away, his equipment at the ready. A young woman with very pale skin, round tortoiseshell glasses, and wildly curly dark hair also hovered nearby. She was wearing an RH News sweatshirt, several shoulder bags, and an anxious expression.

"I guess Marletta was serious about trying the vegetarian chili," Bess remarked with a smile.

At that moment the dark-haired young woman rushed away from the others. A white van with the RH News logo painted on the side was parked just across the street, and as my friends and I watched, the young woman scurried toward it, barely escaping being mowed down by a passing sedan. She quickly climbed inside the van, emerging a moment later carrying yet another bag. Soon she was back, digging into the new bag until she found a makeup tube, which she quickly used to touch up Marletta's face.

"Must be quite a job being Marletta's assistant," I commented.

Bess nodded, but there was no response from George. When I glanced over at her, she had a sour expression on her face, and she was glaring at something behind me. For a second I thought her bad mood had returned. But when I turned around, I quickly realized that this time, there was a very specific reason for George's grumpiness.

"Deirdre Shannon," I whispered, immediately recognizing the pretty, dark-haired girl about my own age who was standing with a group of well-dressed older women near the front of the line. My friends and I have known Deirdre for years, but that doesn't mean we're friends. Far from it.

"We should have known she'd be all over something like this," Bess added, rolling her eyes.

George nodded. "Is it too late to run away before she sees us?" she quipped.

Just then Deirdre glanced up and spotted us staring at her. Stepping out of line with a word to her companions, she strolled toward us.

"Too late," I whispered.

Deirdre reached us and smiled frostily. "Hello, Nancy. Bess. Geor-*gia*." She drew out the last syllable of George's full name, which George hated. Bess and I aren't exactly best friends with Deirdre, but she and George get along about as well as oil and water. "What are *you* three doing *here*?" Deirdre's tone was dripping with a level of incredulity that seemed better suited for a trio of hobos showing up at a black-tie reception.

"What's it to you . . . *DeeDee*?" George retorted, eliciting a scowl from Deirdre, who despises her own childhood nickname just as much as George hates being called by her full name.

I quickly elbowed George in the ribs. As tempting

as it often was to respond to Deirdre's rudeness and snobbery in kind, it was usually better not to antagonize her. That girl could hold a grudge like nobody's business, and being petty is one of her hobbies—along with spending her parents' money, hanging out at the country club, and ordering around her endless and ever-changing parade of boyfriends.

Forcing a pleasant smile onto my face, I answered Deirdre politely. "We just thought we'd come down here and check out the new—"

The rest of my words were swallowed up in a sudden eruption of shouting from somewhere very close by. Glancing around curiously, I saw a small group of people marching toward the front of the spa. Several of them were wearing green T-shirts with a large, stylized oak leaf printed on them, which I recognized as the logo of a local environmental group. In the lead was a scruffy-looking young man with stringy, dirty-blond hair and wild blue eyes. He was holding a sign in one hand and pumping his other fist up and down as he shouted hoarsely at the crowd. I squinted, but couldn't quite make out the words on his sign.

"Isn't that Thomas Rackham?" Bess said.

Deirdre snorted. "Thomas Rackham *Junior*," she corrected disdainfully.

"Uh-oh," George said. "Looks like he's all worked

up about another cause. Wonder what kind of tree frog he wants to save this time?"

Even Deirdre smirked slightly at that. Thomas Rackham Jr. is a peripheral member of the very wealthy family that made their fortune a couple of generations ago through local computer conglomerate Rackham Industries. Thomas Jr. is a few years old than me, and I've met him several times—Dad helped get him out of jail once or twice. Everyone in River Heights knows about Thomas's penchant for getting involved in various radical causes—the more hopeless or obscure, the better.

"Isn't he the guy who chained himself to that half-dead old willow tree in Riverside Park last spring?" George asked.

I nodded. "He was protesting because the city council wanted it cut down before it fell on someone. Dad had to miss his tennis lesson to go bail Thomas out that time," I said. "Come on, let's get closer. I want to see what they're protesting."

As we pushed our way through the crowd, with Deirdre trailing along behind us, I noticed several people eagerly snapping pictures of the protesters. That made me realize that Marletta Michaels wasn't the only person covering the spa's grand opening for the media. I belatedly recognized a newspaper reporter I'd spoken to a few times in the past, as well as at least one field reporter from one of the other local TV stations.

I winced, realizing that Thomas Jr.'s protest probably wasn't the kind of publicity Tessa Monroe had in mind for her grand opening. Even as the thought crossed my mind, I saw Tessa herself hurrying out of the lobby. Even though I'd never met her, it was easy to recognize her from seeing her on TV. She was a tall, beautiful woman in her early thirties with a café-au-lait complexion and sleek dark hair pulled back into a bun. As I watched, the newspaper reporter I'd spotted accosted her.

Meanwhile my friends and I were getting closer to Thomas Rackham Jr. and his companions. Finally I was able to make out the words of their chant: "Down with facials, down with mud. Give the turtles back their 'hood!"

And I was finally able to read Thomas's sign. It featured a picture of a turtle and the words DON'T SHELL OUT MONEY TO SUPPORT HABITAT THEFT!

"Turtles, huh?" George said. She looked around at the area surrounding the spa. The only hint of open, natural space was the park next door. "Um, okay . . ."

I stepped forward and waved at Thomas Jr. "Hi there!" I called between chants, hoping he remembered me.

He turned and squinted in my direction. "Nancy?" he said. "Nancy Drew? Is that you?"

"Hi, Thomas." I smiled at him. "Nice to see you again. What are you guys doing here?"

"We're here to shut this place down!" Thomas puffed out his scrawny chest as he gestured grandly toward the spa. "It's built on the only native habitat of the Middle Midwestern Lesser Spotted Ground Turtle."

"Here? Really?" I looked around dubiously, from paved sidewalk to street light to parking lot. I cleared my throat, trying to be tactful. "Um, are you sure this cause is worth your efforts? I mean, this place is right in the middle of town. I don't think it's likely to be returned to nature anytime soon."

"The turtles have no voice," Thomas replied, his eyes flashing with enthusiasm. "I—we—must be a voice for them! Save the turtles!"

Before I could say anything else, Marletta Michaels burst out of the crowd nearby with her microphone at the ready and her cameraman right behind her. "Excuse me!" she shouted loudly. "Channel RH News, coming through."

"Hey, gotta go," Thomas said to me breathlessly as he saw her coming. He switched his protest sign to the other hand. "See you around, Nancy. Oh, and tell your father I might be calling him later. If things go well. You know." He waved one hand at the police car that had just double-parked nearby—its flashers going—and smiled hopefully.

23

My friends and I moved away as Marletta Michaels rushed toward Thomas and the other protesters from one direction, and the police officers hurried toward him from another. For a moment I thought Deirdre was going to continue trailing after us, but when I glanced over my shoulder I saw her fluffing her dark hair and wetting her lips, and guessed that she was more interested in trying to get herself on TV than in pestering us any longer.

"Hey, look," I said, pointing toward Tessa Monroe, who was standing alone a few yards away near the entrance. She was watching the commotion around Thomas Rackham and his cronies, a worried crease in her smooth forehead. "Want to go try to say hi?"

"Sure," Bess agreed, as George shrugged noncommittally.

I walked toward the spa owner. "Hi there," I said when I reached her. "You don't know me, but I just wanted to—"

"Of course I know you," Tessa interrupted, the worried crease disappearing as her face lit up with a warm smile. She reached out and took my hand in both of her own. "You're Nancy Drew. I recognize you from the pictures in your father's office, and all the newspaper articles, of course. I'm so glad you were able to come down today!"

I blushed slightly as Bess and George grinned. I

24

can face down a hardened criminal or recalcitrant witness without batting an eye, but it's always a little unnerving when regular people recognize me based on my reputation for amateur sleuthing.

"Thanks," I said. I quickly introduced her to Bess and George. "We were all really excited when Dad offered us those free passes you gave him."

"I'm so glad," Tessa said. "I hope you girls will tell me what you think of the—"

"Excuse me!" a shrill voice broke in before Tessa could finish. "Ms. Monroe, could we have another quick word with you, please?"

I thought I detected a slight, weary sigh as Tessa turned to face Marletta Michaels, who was rushing toward her with her entourage in tow.

"Of course, Ms. Michaels," Tessa said politely. "As long as it is a quick one. I need to get back inside soon."

Marletta nodded briskly, then glanced at her cameraman to make sure he was filming her. She held up her microphone. "I'm standing here with Tessa Monroe, owner and manager of Indulgences Spa," she said into the camera. She turned to face Tessa. "Ms. Monroe, would you care to comment on the protest going on outside your business right now? Apparently some local environmentalists are concerned that the spa is taking away valuable habitat from an endangered species of turtle."

I barely contained a laugh. Somehow, Thomas Rackham and his motley crew hardly seemed to deserve the description *environmentalists.*

"I'm all in favor of environmental causes, of course," Tessa replied calmly. "However, this spa was built on a site that has been developed for well over seventy-five years—most recently as the old Carr candy factory. So I'm not sure this particular protest has much merit from a practical standpoint, though of course I wish them well in their quest to save endangered species." She nodded politely toward Marletta. "Now, if you'll excuse me, I'm afraid I must run. I need to go around back and check on the bottled water delivery."

Marletta tried to stop her with more rapid-fire questions, but Tessa didn't look back as she strode away toward the lobby. "Fine," the reporter muttered, sounding slightly irritated. "Lulu, did you get the rest of the quote from that young woman in the penguin T-shirt?"

"I think so, Marletta," the frantic-looking young assistant replied breathlessly. "I've got it right here somewhere. . . ."

My friends and I watched for a few minutes as the reporter and her team shot some additional footage of Marletta. Then, out of the corner of my eye, I suddenly spotted Deirdre heading in our direction once again, looking very smug. I decided it was probably a good time to make ourselves scarce.

"Let's get out of here," I muttered to my friends, nudging them and nodding toward Deirdre. "I have a feeling our day will be much more pleasant if we try to avoid you–know–who as much as possible."

"Good plan," George said immediately.

Bess nodded. "Maybe we could duck into the lobby," she suggested. "I mean, with those passes your dad gave us, we should be able to skip to the front of the line, right?"

"I have a better idea." George grabbed her arm and dragged her toward the corner of the building. I followed.

Soon we found ourselves walking down the narrow alley between the spa's stucco wall and the chain-link fence separating the property from the park next door. As soon as we were out of sight of the crowd out front—especially Deirdre—we all relaxed and slowed our pace.

"Okay," I said, glancing over at George. "So now what?"

George shrugged. "I don't know," she said. "I thought it might be fun to check out the grounds of this place before we go inside."

"That's a good idea," Bess said. "I heard there's a meditation garden in the back. We could try to get a look at that. Maybe then the lines will die down and we can head inside."

I shrugged agreeably. "Let's go, then."

I led the way toward the back corner of the building. We were only a few feet away when the sound of angry voices suddenly erupted from somewhere around the corner.

". . . and if you weren't so stinkin' greedy, we wouldn't have this problem!" a man's voice was exclaiming loudly.

"Just calm down, okay?" a woman's voice responded, sounding much calmer. "Let's talk about this like adults."

"Hey, isn't that Tessa?" Bess whispered, her blue eyes wide.

I nodded, easily recognizing the spa owner's melodious voice. I also recognized the anger in her companion's voice, and it worried me. When people sound like that, it usually means trouble. Concerned for Tessa, I leaned forward so I could hear better. But I shouldn't have bothered. The unknown man's voice burst out again, loud enough to make us all jump a little.

"I'm done trying to talk to you, Tessa!" he shouted furiously. "And mark my words. By the time I get through with you, you won't be able to shut down this stupid place fast enough!"

3

A Meaty Mistake

Before any of us could react to what we'd just heard, the sound of rushing footsteps approached from around the corner. A second later Tessa burst into view, her cheeks flushed and her dark eyes flashing angrily.

She stopped short when she saw us. "Oh," she said. "Hello, girls." She sighed, taking in our shocked expressions. "I suppose you overheard that just now?"

Bess was the first one to find her voice. "It's okay," she said quickly. "You don't have to explain anything to us. We didn't mean to eavesdrop."

Tessa shrugged. "It's all right," she said. "That was just my hateful—and loud—ex-husband, Dan." She tugged on a stray strand of dark hair that had fallen over her face. "He's always had a temper, which was always part of our problem. . . . But anyway, he's still angry because he didn't get away with grabbing the lion's share of our assets in the divorce. That's mostly thanks to your father, Nancy. He represented me." She managed a small smile.

I blinked in surprise. Somehow, when Dad had mentioned representing Tessa, I had assumed it had something to do with the spa—working out some kind of real estate contract or business license, perhaps. I couldn't help feeling slightly annoyed with myself for jumping to conclusions. A good detective should know better than that.

Not that it mattered. It's not like I was on the trail of any mysteries at that moment. It was just supposed to be a relaxing day at the spa.

"Anyway," Tessa continued, "now that I've opened this new business without him, he's threatening to sue for a share of the profits. Or maybe he really just wants to tangle me up in so many legal fees that I have to shut down. Who knows? I'm not going to waste one more second worrying about him, though."

I bit my lip, remembering the white-hot anger in Dan's voice. "Are you sure you don't want to, you know, talk to the police or something? They're right out front."

Tessa smiled. "Don't worry," she assured me. "Dan won't dare to actually cause any real trouble. He's a coward at heart. He mostly just wants to make sure I don't actually enjoy myself today. That's the only reason he showed up here."

I nodded, accepting what she was saying for the most part. After all, she knew her ex-husband best. Still, I couldn't stop a bit of worry from taking hold in my mind. Thanks to some of the mysteries I've solved in the past, I've learned that sometimes cowards can be the most dangerous enemies of all.

Tessa checked her watch. "Have you girls been inside yet?" she asked. When we shook our heads, she smiled. "Come with me, then. I'll make sure you get the VIP treatment."

A few minutes later we were walking into the crowded lobby at Tessa's side. About halfway to the front desk, she paused to say hello to several people waiting in the line to get in, which stretched out the door and halfway down the block by now. As we stood waiting for Tessa to finish and continue on inside, I noticed Deirdre standing in line a few people back. She stared at us in obvious surprise.

George spotted her too. "Yoo-hoo!" she called cheerfully, waving to the other girl. "Hi there, Deirdre. Still waiting in that line, are you? Too bad." She shook her head in mock pity. "Guess we'll see you inside—whenever you make it in."

For once Deirdre seemed to be speechless. She just

glared at us, her cheeks slowly turning pink with fury.

Even though I usually try not to encourage George when she and Deirdre start sniping at each other, I couldn't hide a grin as Tessa finished her conversation and we swept on past the rest of the line and into the spa.

For the next hour or so my friends and I enjoyed a wide sampling of the luxuries the spa had to offer. Or at least, Bess and I thoroughly enjoyed it. When she wasn't gloating about dissing Deirdre on our way in, George seemed a little jumpy—she couldn't quite go with the Indulgences flow and just relax. But at least she wasn't in her cranky mood from the day before.

Upon arrival we were shown to a locker room and given soft, organic cotton gowns with fluffy robes to go over them. We also traded in our shoes and socks for a pair of comfy slippers. At first it felt strange to walk around in public like that, but everyone else around us was wearing the same thing. After several hours of mud scrubs, face peels, and organic carrot juice, we found ourselves lying face down on comfortable tables in a semiprivate room in the massage wing. Three pleasant, uniformed masseuses worked on our muscles while classical music played softly in the background and the scents of vanilla and lemongrass perfumed the air.

"Aah," Bess murmured contentedly, her voice muffled slightly by the pillow of her massage table. "This is the life, isn't it?"

"Totally," I agreed sleepily, turning my head to look over at her. Meanwhile the woman working on my shoulder muscles never paused in her rhythmic motion, which was so soothing that I felt as if I could lie there enjoying it forever.

Out of the corner of my eye, I saw George's masseuse straighten up. "There you go, Miss Fayne," she said politely. "I hope that was satisfactory?"

"Sure, thanks." George sat up abruptly as her masseuse backed away. "Okay, we've done the facial-and-manicure thing, and tasted more kinds of wheat-grass than I knew existed, and had our auras waxed or whatever they were supposed to be doing to us in that last room," she said, ticking off each activity on a finger. "And now the massage thing. Guess that means we're about ready to cut out of here, huh?"

Bess turned her head to look at George. "No way!" she protested lazily. "We still haven't been to the Roman mud bath room, remember?"

With some effort I lifted my arm just enough to glance at my watch. "Our appointment is at three."

Just then Bess's masseuse finished as well, followed by mine. Reluctantly I sat up and stretched.

"Thanks, Wendy," I said to my masseuse. "That was awesome!"

Wendy smiled. "You're quite welcome, Miss Drew," she said. "I hope you'll come back again soon."

The three women headed out of the room to let us dress. As George slipped on her robe, I noticed she was frowning. "So we have to hang around here until three o'clock?" she said. "It's not even noon now. Hey, Tessa said we're VIPs, right? Maybe we could see if there's any chance of moving it up a couple of hours. Then we can get out of here sooner."

"Why?" Bess said with a slight frown. "There's still plenty to do before we go. We haven't tried the steam room yet, or checked out the restaurant. . . ."

Bess and George were still bickering as we stepped out of the massage room into the main hallway and almost ran smack into Marletta Michaels and her cameraman. The cameraman was still dressed in his street clothes, but Marletta was wearing an Indulgences robe and slippers. The pair was being trailed by a couple of uniformed spa employees. I was surprised to see the reporter still hanging around. The last time I'd walked past the lobby, I'd noticed that most of the media people seemed to have packed up and left. However Thomas Rackham and the other protesters were still outside, with a solitary police car keeping watch over them. I wondered if Marletta was trying to use the protest to turn the spa opening into a more interesting story.

"Hello, ladies," Marletta said to us with a pleasant smile. "Please excuse the interruption." She blinked, staring at me intently. "Hey, aren't you Nancy Drew? I interviewed you last year, didn't I?"

"Yes, that's right. Nice to see you again." She had actually interviewed me more than once after I'd solved some local crime or other, but it didn't really matter.

"Yes, lovely," Marletta responded breezily. "I was just wondering if you and your friends here would be willing to give a few comments about your experience here? I'd love to have a few firsthand reviews to put on the air with my story about the grand opening."

"Sure," Bess said with a dimpled smile. "George just loves to be on TV, and . . ."

Her voice trailed off as she frowned and looked over my shoulder. Glancing in that direction, I quickly realized why: George was just disappearing around the corner at the end of the hall. If she had been a cartoon character, there would have been a little puff of dust kicking up behind her slippers.

"Oops," I said. "Guess that's a no from George." I smiled apologetically at the reporter. "But Bess and

I wouldn't mind saying a few words about this place . . . especially after the fabulous massages we just had."

"Terrific." Marletta glanced around, her smile fading slightly. "Where is that girl when I need her?" she muttered. "Oh, well. Frank, how's my hair?"

"Looks good, boss," the cameraman said with the same enthusiasm he might use to observe that the sky was still blue. He switched on his camera and started taping.

Marletta touched her tall blond pouf of hair tentatively, then shrugged, raised her microphone, and pasted a brilliant smile onto her face. "Hello, River Heights," she said, her voice taking on a bright, chipper tone. "I'm here with some young ladies who are enjoying a day of pampering at the newly opened Indulgences Spa. . . ."

She finished her introductory patter, then had Bess and me introduce ourselves before asking us a few questions about our activities so far that day. We answered as best we could. I can't speak for Bess, but I had a hard time keeping a straight face while answering serious questions about the quality of the seaweed I'd had patted onto my face.

Finally Marletta seemed to be winding down. "Sounds like you're having a wonderful day," she said brightly. "I do hope you're planning to try the restaurant before you go. It's an all-vegetarian menu, you know."

Bess giggled. "We know," she said. "George—that's our friend who just left—has been complaining about it all day."

"Oh?" Marletta frowned slightly. "Does that mean she's not a vegetarian?"

I shrugged. "None of us are, actually," I said. "But we're still definitely looking forward to trying the—"

"How can you be so casual about your own carnivorous habits?" Marletta interrupted, her perky smile fading. "You look like such intelligent young women. Haven't you figured out yet that meat is killing our Earth through factory farming?"

"Easy, boss," the cameraman murmured under his breath.

Marletta shot him a withering glance before returning her full attention to us. "Don't you girls know about the connection between beef farming and the destruction of the rain forest?" she demanded. "I suggest that you look up the study that found that over seventy-five percent of—"

"All right, then," one of the spa employees, a pleasant-looking middle-aged woman, interrupted firmly. She stepped forward. "I think we've taken up enough of these lovely young ladies' time. Thanks so much for helping out, and please allow Indulgences to thank you with a free dessert at lunch . . . on us. Just tell your waitress Janine said so." The employee smiled apologetically at us, rolling her eyes as soon as Marletta's back was turned.

I winked at her in return. "Thanks, though it's quite all right," I said. "We were glad to help."

"But I wanted to ask them about . . . ," Marletta began irritably, but the rest of her words were lost as the employee dragged her off down the hall, politely scolding her for harassing their customers. The cameraman shrugged, switched off his camera, and followed them.

"Well, that was interesting," I said with a laugh as soon as they were out of earshot. "Too bad George missed it. I'm sure she would have come up with something good after that beef farming line."

Bess didn't respond for a moment. "Speaking of George, have you noticed she's acting a little weird today?" she asked at last. "I mean, weird even for her being at a spa, you know."

I nodded, knowing she was referring to her cousin's recent disappearing act. "Trust me, I've noticed," I said. "But it actually started yesterday, remember? She was so down on coming here. At first I thought it was just the usual reason—"

Bess rolled her eyes and nodded. "Me too," she said. "I know she's been totally broke for the past couple of weeks, and she really needs cash to pay for a special present for our grandmother's seventy-fifth birthday coming up. I figured that was why she was being so snarky about this place." She shrugged. "But then your dad turned up with the free passes, and I figured, problem solved."

"I know," I said. "And George seemed a little more chipper this morning, but . . ."

I shook my head, wondering if I'd been ignoring a true mystery in the making right under my nose. Why hadn't I paid attention until now? George's behavior was just a little too strange to attribute to her perpetual lack of cash or her general disdain for Bess's brand of *über*girly fun.

Bess shrugged. "So what do we do?"

"I guess the first thing we need to do is find her," I said. "Why don't we split up and do a quick search? We can meet back here in like, twenty minutes."

Bess agreed and we parted ways. I quickly checked a few likely spots—the nearest restroom, the gift shop, the lap pool. But George was nowhere to be found.

By then the twenty minutes were almost up. As I wandered through the hair care wing, trying to decide whether to check some of the rooms there before going back to meet Bess, I noticed the scent of delicious-smelling food wafting down the hallway.

"Aha," I murmured. "Food!"

George loves to eat, and it was almost lunchtime. As much as she liked to complain about the vegetarian menu, I suspected she would be happy to follow her nose—and her stomach—to the spa's restaurant.

Following my own nose, I wound my way through the maze of hallways, searching for the source of the delicious scent. Finally I found my way to a door marked EMPLOYEES ONLY PLEASE. Peeking through it, I saw an empty hallway beyond. I stepped through and looked around. This section of the spa was as clean and quiet as the rest of the place, though it lacked the soft lighting and framed floral prints of the public areas. The scent of cooking was stronger here. Walking down the hall, I soon came to a wide doorway and, based on the smell, realized it had to be the kitchen. I cautiously poked my head in through the swinging doors.

"Hello?" I called. "Anybody here?"

There was no answer. I glanced around the large, well-lit, nearly spotless kitchen. Several large stovetops held pots and pans of various sizes, while sliced vegetables and toast sizzled quietly on an indoor grill. The only odd thing about the scene was the absence of people. I guessed that the chef must have stepped out for a moment.

I was about to back away from the door, but just

then my stomach let out a hungry rumble. The scent of blending juices and spices was almost intoxicating, and I couldn't resist peeking to see what sort of vegetarian dish could possibly be emitting that heavenly smell—whatever it was, I wanted to be sure to order it. Using my best detective skills, I soon traced the scent to a particular large stew pot bubbling merrily away on one of the enormous stainless steel stoves.

"Mmm," I murmured, closing my eyes and taking a deep breath of the steam rising out of the pot. "No wonder the smell pulled me in here. Smells just like Dad's Triple-Beef Superchili."

My eyes flew open and I frowned. Wait a minute—Triple-Beef Superchili? In a totally vegetarian restaurant?

"No way," I whispered to myself with a rueful smile. "Guess it must just be an incredible simulation of that smell."

I started to back away. But something made me take another step forward instead. By standing on tiptoes, I could just barely see over the edge of the pot into the boiling stew inside. I could see beans, celery, carrots, along with plenty of chunks of something that looked suspiciously like . . . beef.

Maybe it's some kind of tofu-based meat substitute? I speculated uncertainly.

I don't think I've mentioned my hunches yet.

When I'm on the trail of something suspicious, I sometimes get a weird, tingly sort of feeling in my gut that leads me to a breakthrough or a clue. Dad says it's just my knowledge of the case combined with a little bit of detective's intuition. Bess says I have a sixth sense about weird stuff. George just calls it freaky.

In any case I was having one of those hunches now, and it told me I'd better take a quick look around, because something about this seemingly peaceful scene just didn't add up. I glanced into a few of the pots on nearby burners and found nothing more suspicious than a weird-looking type of vegetable I'd never seen before. Noticing that the handle of each cooking pot was adorned with a handwritten label, I saw that the mystery veggie was something called cardoons.

Just then I noticed a large trash bin tucked into a corner near the door. It was full to overflowing, and I saw that a couple of boxes had fallen on the floor. I took a step toward the bin, squinting at the corner of a white foam package poking out from among the other trash. When I got closer, my eyes widened as I spotted the reddish juices dripping off the edge of the foam tray—and the printed label that read USDA GRADE A BEEF.

4

More Trouble

quickly double-checked the label on the stew pot, just to make sure I hadn't misunderstood Marletta's comments earlier. Maybe the spa's restaurant wasn't strictly vegetarian after all—maybe it offered one or two alternative dishes for meat-eating customers, the way many regular restaurants provided a vegetarian choice.

But no. In bold print, the label on the pot read VEGETARIAN CHILI.

As mysteries went, what I'd just discovered hardly qualified as murder or mayhem. But I immediately recognized how damaging this could be for Tessa's business if word got out—especially with Marletta Michaels still lurking around outside looking for story material.

I was still trying to figure out what to do a few seconds later when a short, plump woman burst into the room through the door leading out the back of the kitchen, muttering irritably under her breath and shaking her head. She had a round, rosy-cheeked face, thick dark curls barely held in check by a hardworking hairnet, and a name tag reading PATSY on the lapel of her white coat. She blinked when she noticed me standing by the stove. "Oh, hello. Are you lost? The spa's back that way." She pointed to the door through which I'd entered.

"My name is Nancy Drew," I said, stepping forward. "Are you the head chef? Because there's something I think you ought to see."

Patsy looked confused. "But where did you come from, Nancy?" she asked. "I just stepped out back five minutes ago. . . ." Her cheerful face rearranged itself into a frown, though it wasn't directed at me. "Of course, it would have been helpful if the lettuce delivery was actually there waiting for me, like that girl said."

The chef seemed more than a little distracted. But when I directed her attention into the stew pot, she immediately gasped with shock. "What's this?" she cried, grabbing a ladle from a shelf nearby and scooping up some of the chili. "Did you do this? Did you put this—this—*meat* in here while I was gone?" She pronounced the word *meat* the way some people might say *poison*.

"No, no!" I assured her. "I just walked in a moment ago myself. But I noticed the smell, and went to look into the pot—" I quickly did my best to explain what had happened.

Patsy dropped the ladle and grasped her hair with both hands, nearly ripping off her hairnet. "But it was perfect when I stepped out!" she wailed, tears springing to her round blue eyes as she stared into the pot. "Who could have done this? Oh, if Tessa thinks I messed up, she'll have my head—especially after what happened last week!"

"What happened last week?" I asked curiously.

Patsy blinked and stared at me, as if just remembering I was there. "Oh," she said. "It was just something at a pre-opening meeting for all the employees." She shrugged. "The kitchen wasn't quite finished yet, so we were supposed to bring a brown-bag lunch. One of the girls brought a turkey sandwich, and from the way Tessa reacted, you would've thought it was a bomb or something!" The chef's eyes grew even rounder at the recollection. "She started yelling something about how even having meat on the property would reflect on our vegetarian credibility. You know, for the publicity or what have you. So Tessa fired the girl."

"Wow," I commented. I could hardly imagine mild-mannered Tessa reacting like that to something so minor.

"Don't get me wrong," Patsy continued quickly. "It was hardly this girl's first offense. She was trouble from the start—always late, sneaking around against the rules, that kind of thing. But still . . ." She gazed woefully into the stew pot.

I learned long ago that people will say or do just about anything to cover up their wrongdoings. And I know that one of the most likely suspects in any sort of trouble is the person with the easiest access to the scene of the crime. That meant Patsy had to be considered a suspect. But I've also learned to trust my own judgments of people, and I had a feeling that the chef was at least as surprised at seeing meat in the chili as I was. Besides, what could possibly be her motive to do such a thing?

Suspects, motives, the scene of the crime . . . I realized that thinking that way had just made it official—I'd found yet another mystery!

At that moment a couple of other kitchen workers entered, and soon they were all moaning and fretting together over the chili. I took advantage of their distraction to take a quick look around for clues.

Aside from the meat package in the trash bin, there didn't seem to be much out of the ordinary as far as I could tell. It was easy to tell that Patsy liked to keep her work area clean—I couldn't even see any fingerprints on the shiny metal edges of the stove. But as I was turning away a second later, I caught a flash of something out of place on the smooth stainless steel surface of the stove front. Leaning down for a better look, I saw what appeared to be a clump of hair caught in one of the knobs. Wrinkling my nose with disgust, I forced myself to grab it for a better look. Yep, it was hair all right—long, blond, straight hair. I glanced over at the chef's dark curls. This hair definitely hadn't come from her head.

". . . have to get Tessa."

I realized I'd completely tuned out Patsy's rantings. "Er, what?"

"Tessa," Patsy repeated frantically as one of the other workers hurried out of the kitchen. "She's going to be horrified."

The chef was right. When the owner arrived a few minutes later and heard what had happened, her eyes immediately went wide with horror. "But how could this happen?" she exclaimed.

Patsy let out a sob. "I swear, I had nothing to do with it!" she cried. "Please, Tessa, you have to believe me."

Tessa reached over and gave the chef a quick, sympathetic pat on the shoulder. But the chef hardly seemed to be listening. Instead she cast a nervous glance toward the doors. "Quick," Tessa whispered hoarsely, grabbing a lid off the rack above the stove and jamming it onto the pot. "We have to get this out of here before someone—"

"Yoo-hoo! Anybody home?" a bright, peppy voice called from the doorway.

I glanced over my shoulder and gulped. It was Marletta Michaels, trailed as usual by her cameraman and assistant.

Tessa's face froze momentarily. But a split second later she was hurrying forward, smiling serenely at the reporter. "Hello, Marletta," she said, her voice sounding as calm as ever.

She put one hand on the other woman's arm, subtly managing to turn her so that they were both facing away from the chili pot. Meanwhile the chef quickly stuffed the pot into an empty oven and frantically fanned at the air with an oven mitt, obviously trying to dissipate the meaty scent. The other kitchen workers hurried forward and surrounded the cameraman and assistant, clearly trying to distract them.

"What are you doing here?" Tessa asked Marletta pleasantly. "I thought you were in the mud room."

"I was," Marletta replied. "But a little bird told me I should come to the kitchen right away to find a big news story."

Tessa looked startled. My eyes narrowed. Something was smelling a little funny about this whole situation, and it wasn't the beef chili.

"A little bird?" I repeated, stepping forward. "What do you mean? Who told you to come here right now?"

Marletta blinked at me. "Oh, it's you again," she said. She shrugged. "It was my assistant—she overheard something about it, I think. Lulu!" she called. "Over here, please."

The young, dark-haired assistant hurried over, the hem of her Indulgences robe flapping. "What is it, Marletta?" she asked breathlessly. "Did you figure out what the big story is yet?"

"Not quite," Marletta replied. "Tell me again, Lulu. What exactly made you think something was going on in here?"

Lulu shrugged one thin shoulder uncertainly. "I was in the bathroom a few minutes ago," she said. "A couple of other women came in and started whispering. All I heard was something about trouble, and the kitchen, and a big scandal." She wet her lips, looking anxious. "I tried to hurry out and find out more, but by the time I got out of the stall, they were gone."

"Did you notice anything about their voices?" I asked. "You said there were two women, right? Did either of them have an accent or any kind of unusual voice—very high, very low, anything like that?"

Lulu blinked at me from behind her glasses, looking confused. "No, I didn't notice anything like that," she said. "Um, who are you? Do you work here?"

Before I could answer, I heard footsteps at the kitchen door. Turning, I saw Bess and George step in.

"Nancy!" Bess cried. "There you are. We've been looking all over for you."

I opened my mouth to answer. Before I could, I saw George glance around the room, then spin on her heel and disappear back through the door. Huh.

But right now, I couldn't really think about my friend's odd behavior. I had to stay much more concerned with what had just happened in the spa kitchen. I quickly excused myself from Tessa and the others.

"Come here a sec," I whispered, grabbing Bess by the arm and dragging her to a private corner of the kitchen near the door.

I glanced around to make sure we wouldn't be overheard. Marletta and her assistant were still talking with Tessa. Nearby the cameraman was chatting with one of the kitchen workers. Patsy and another worker were busy at the stove. There was no sign of the beef chili, and even the smell had dissipated quite a bit.

"What's going on?" Bess asked. "And where's

George? I thought she was right behind me."

"Never mind her," I whispered. "Listen . . ."

I quickly filled her in. Her eyes widened when I mentioned seeing the meat packages in the trash, and her gaze wandered toward the garbage bin. I looked over that way too, and saw that Patsy or one of the others had tossed a large cardboard box atop the bin, effectively hiding everything underneath.

"Wow," Bess said when I finished. "Bad luck that Marletta came in just now. But what's the big deal? I'm sure it was just a mistake. Someone tossed that beef into the wrong pot or whatever."

I shook my head. "Think about it," I said. "What would packages of beef be doing in a totally vegetarian kitchen in the first place?"

"Oh." Bess shrugged. "Good point."

I paused before replying, noticing that Marletta's assistant, Lulu, was hurrying in our direction. But she didn't even glance at us. Instead she rushed past and out of the room. Judging by the anxious expression on her pale face, I guessed that Marletta had sent her on some kind of urgent errand. I just hoped she wasn't still trying to figure out what "big news" might be happening in the kitchen at the moment. . . .

"I'm also not sure it's a coincidence that Marletta turned up just now," I told Bess when we were alone again. "Her assistant heard someone talking in the restroom, and I wonder if—"

"This is an outrage!"

I jumped as the loud, commanding voice burst out from the doorway nearby. Spinning around, I saw Deirdre standing there, looking red faced and furious. She was dressed in one of the spa's robes, though she was wearing a pair of beaded silk slippers that I guessed had to be her own. She also had a towel wrapped around her hair.

"Oh, man. What's *she* doing here?" Bess muttered as Deirdre stormed toward Tessa. She blinked. "Cute slippers," I heard her add under her breath.

"I don't know," I said, rolling my eyes. "But as usual, she has impeccable timing. The last thing Tessa needs right now is some typical Deirdre Shannon temper tantrum because the hair conditioner wasn't the right brand or something."

Bess was still staring at Deirdre. "Or maybe she's complaining about whatever they put on her face," she said. "She looks like a tomato."

Whatever the reason for Deirdre's sudden interruption, I couldn't help feeling irritated with her for storming in and causing a scene in front of the reporter. I just hoped that Tessa could work her magic and soothe Deirdre before she made a scene—and that Marletta would get bored with the kitchen nonstory and start concocting a story out of Deirdre instead. Maybe something like NEW SPA TURNS LOCAL GIRL INTO HUMAN LOBSTER!

Deirdre didn't even seem to notice Bess and me standing there as she stomped past us and stopped short in front of Tessa, her hands on her hips as she glared at the spa owner. "I want to talk to you!" she exclaimed loudly.

"Yes, of course. Just a moment, please." Tessa's face had turned slightly pale, but she maintained her pleasant smile as she turned toward Marletta. "I'm sure this will only take a moment, and then I can show you around some more. In the meantime why don't you have Patsy let you sample some of the dishes for today's lunch? You'll be the first in town to taste her delicious specialties."

Marletta looked pleased at that, though she cast a curious look at Deirdre. "All right," she said.

Patsy hurried over at Tessa's summons, and soon she and Marletta were pouring samples onto tasting plates on the other side of the kitchen. The cameraman followed, looking hungry.

Meanwhile Bess and I drifted closer to Tessa and Deirdre. I was still pondering the meat mystery, trying to figure out what it all meant. Why would someone sabotage the chili that way? It seemed like an odd way to cause trouble. Even if I hadn't happened upon it, I was sure that Patsy would have discovered the problem as soon as she'd returned from her errand, so it wasn't as if there was much chance of the meat-laced chili actually being served to Tessa's customers. If Marletta's assistant hadn't overheard that conversation in the ladies' room, it was unlikely that anyone but the staff ever would have known that something was going on. It didn't seem to make sense—unless the meat was supposed to be some kind of warning or threat to Tessa.

I was thinking so hard that I wasn't paying much attention as Deirdre started ranting at Tessa. The only words I caught at first were *pedicure* and *steam room*.

Then I heard Bess gasp. I glanced over at her. "What?" I asked.

". . . and I could have been killed!" Deirdre cried.

"Wait," I said, stepping toward her. "Hold on. What's going on? What happened to you, Deirdre?"

My presence in the kitchen finally registered on Deirdre's bright red face. She scowled at me, but answered my question.

"I just said," she ranted. "I was in one of the private steam rooms, relaxing after my pedicure. While I was in there, I noticed it was getting hot—really hot. I went outside and found out why. Someone turned up the thermostat by thirty degrees while I was inside!"

54

5

Joining Forces

"I **could have boiled** to death!" Deirdre complained, returning her attention to Tessa.

The spa owner looked alarmed. "I'm so sorry, Miss Shannon," she said quickly. "I—I don't know how that could have happened. The temperatures in the saunas are supposed to stay put. But I assure you, we'll do everything we can to make it up to you, if we can just step out into the hall and discuss it. . . ."

For a second Deirdre looked stubborn, and I was afraid she was going to refuse. I looked across the kitchen just in time to see Marletta glance curiously in our direction. I was getting a very strong feeling that there was something strange going on at the spa, and I wanted a chance to figure out what it was before the story was splashed all over the evening news. I needed Marletta to stay where she was

Finally Deirdre let out a loud sigh. "Well, I suppose I could give you one more chance," she said grudgingly. "But only because Mother likes you." She glanced at me. "Tessa is a member of the River Heights Garden League, you know. And, of course, I'm sure you know Mother is their cofounder and treasurer."

I had to fight to keep from rolling my eyes. The Garden League is one of the snootiest organizations in town. They hold a couple of big, splashy charity events each year to raise money for the city's parks, and meet once a month or so, supposedly to talk about plants. However, I'm not sure how accurate it is to call it a gardening club. I'm pretty sure most of the members have never put their expensively manicured fingers near dirt in their lives.

"I appreciate that," Tessa told Deirdre sincerely. "Come on, let's step outside, shall we?"

I cast a glance across the kitchen as Tessa hustled Deirdre out into the hall. Marletta stayed put, but once again she was looking curiously over at us.

"Uh-oh, looks like she might be about to come over here and start snooping," I murmured to Bess. "Want to go distract her while I help Tessa with Deirdre?"

Bess nodded. "I'm on it," she said. Straightening

her robe, she strode across the room with a bright smile lighting up her face.

I smiled too. Bess has a special knack for distracting people. For the male half of the population, all it usually takes is a toss of her blond hair and that dimpled smile. But even women tend to fall for her naturally sweet and charming personality.

Leaving Marletta and company in Bess's capable hands, I hurried into the hall. Tessa and Deirdre were nowhere in sight in the employees' hallway, but I soon found them just outside in the public area, standing in front of a framed mirror hung over a small table. Deirdre was staring at herself in the mirror, dabbing at her face with a damp corner of the towel wrapped around her head, while Tessa talked to her soothingly.

They both glanced up as I approached. "Do you mind?" Deirdre snapped. "This is a private conversation."

I ignored her. "Tessa," I said, "I have a question for you. It's a little personal, but it could be very important."

Tessa looked surprised, but she nodded agreeably. "I've heard about your reputation, of course, Nancy," she said. "And I guess it's starting to look like I may need your help. One weird accident is one thing, but . . ." She glanced quickly from Deirdre back toward the kitchen hallway before returning her attention to me. "So ask away."

"It's about your ex-husband," I said. "He's the one we accidentally overheard you arguing with earlier, right?"

"Dan?" Tessa shrugged. "What about him?"

"Well, you said he's mad about your divorce, and that he might like to see you go out of business," I said. "You didn't seem too worried about it, but now that this has happened, do you think he could actually be trying to sabotage you?"

Tessa chuckled. "Not a chance," she replied. "Everyone on my staff knows him by sight. If he'd set foot inside the spa today, I would know about it."

While I didn't doubt that Tessa's employees would report any ex-husband sightings, the spa wasn't exactly Fort Knox. I suspected that Tessa's ex could sneak in if he really wanted to—or send someone else in to do his dirty work.

Thinking of that clump of blond hair I'd found in the kitchen, I realized I didn't have any idea what Dan looked like. "Okay," I told Tessa, "but I just have one more quick question about him. What color is his hair?"

"His hair?" Tessa was starting to sound a little distracted. "Funny you should ask. He's forever telling anyone who will listen that he's a natural blond. He's quite vain about his hair, in fact." She looked confused, as if finally realizing it was a rather odd question. "Why do you ask?"

Deirdre was still busy with her own reflection. At that moment she glanced at us over her shoulder. "Uh, excuse me, victim here," she complained. "I'm the one with the fourth-degree face burn, remember?"

"Of course, Deirdre," Tessa replied, rolling her eyes so only I could see. "I haven't forgotten you at all. I really want to make this up to you. In fact, I was just going to offer you a pair of free passes so you and a friend can come back again soon. And of course we'll refund the money you paid for today's visit and provide lunch for you and the rest of your party on the house."

Deirdre looked slightly mollified by that. "Well, I should *hope* so," she muttered.

I was already thinking of more questions, but the spa owner looked distracted. "Now if you two will excuse me, I really should go check on that steam room and make sure someone gives the temperature gauge a good going over," she said anxiously. "After all, there's still a chance this whole thing might have been an accident. . . ."

She didn't sound too convinced about that, and neither was I. As Tessa had mentioned, one weird thing happening could be written off as bad luck.

But two, so close together? Perhaps it was a coincidence, but in my experience, a strange coincidence is always worth a closer look.

Tessa hurried off in the direction of the steam rooms, leaving me standing alone in the hallway with Deirdre. I found myself staring at her, thinking about her steam room story. Deirdre was once again completely focused on her own face, which was finally starting to fade from bright red to a sort of medium fuchsia shade.

Poor Tessa. Bad luck that someone like Deirdre was in the sauna when the saboteur struck. Some people might have handled the problem discreetly, but Deirdre was practically guaranteed to raise a big stink whenever she was even slightly inconvenienced.

I blinked. Wait a minute. What if it wasn't bad luck at all? What if Deirdre had turned up the temperature in the sauna herself, hoping to score lifetime free spa passes or something?

I quickly shook off that idea. While I wouldn't put it past Deirdre to be sneaky or manipulative for her own benefit, there was no way she would risk her precious alabaster skin just to save a few bucks. Besides, it wouldn't explain the chili trick, for which she would have neither an obvious motive nor, at least in my opinion, the creative energy.

No, there was something going on that was a lot

bigger than Deirdre, and I was determined to get to the bottom of it. I just hoped I could figure it out before Tessa's grand opening was ruined.

I continued staring at Deirdre, not really seeing her, as I went over the facts in my mind. Finally, though, she glanced up and noticed my gaze.

"What's your problem?" she said rudely. "Haven't you ever seen someone with a decent haircut before?"

As an insult, it didn't even make sense. For one thing, I'd seen Deirdre lots of times, so if her haircut was so great she should have known I'd already be quite familiar with it. Besides, the towel wrapped around her head was pretty much hiding the evidence either way. But then again, logic has never been a strong suit for Deirdre. I was about to leave her alone with her red-faced reflection and bad mood and return to the kitchen. I figured Bess might have some insight into how to go about investigating at the spa without raising suspicion among the customers, since the whole manicure-and-facial thing was much more her cup of tea than mine.

Then I stopped short, realizing there was one person who was even more knowledgeable about such matters than Bess. And that person was standing right in front of me.

I gulped, a little horrified by the idea that had

suddenly popped into my head. It had just occurred to me that Deirdre could actually be of some help to me for a change. Aside from dating and shopping, pampering herself was definitely her favorite activity, so the luxurious spa was practically her natural environment. Besides, she probably knew most of the customers who were there that day—probably seventy-five percent of them belonged to the country club, or the Garden League, or any of the other groups that attracted the wealthy elite of River Heights along with Deirdre's parents. And unlike me, Deirdre isn't known for asking nosy questions for any reason other than idle gossip, so she would be able to snoop around without raising suspicions that anything might be going wrong at the spa. The more I thought about it, the more sense my idea made.

There was one major problem, of course. This new plan of mine would mean voluntarily spending more time with Deirdre. Was I really desperate enough to inflict that on myself and my friends?

I grimaced, imagining what George's reaction would be. Then I remembered that I hadn't even seen George in a good half hour or more, except for her brief appearance in the kitchen doorway. Even without her input, though, I wasn't sure that Deirdre's help would be worth the trouble.

Before I could decide one way or the other, Deirdre finally stepped away from the mirror. "Oh, well," she said. "Guess I'll go look into that free lunch now."

"Wait," I blurted out as she started to turn away.

She paused, glancing back at me. Her face was nearly back to normal now, just a faint pink blush giving away what had happened.

"What?" she demanded impatiently.

I took a deep breath, still not sure what I wanted to do. "Listen, I was just thinking," I began hesitantly. "Um, that is, it looks like Tessa is in some trouble here. Because of what happened to you, and, you know, some other stuff."

Deirdre was starting to look confused as well as impatient. "Do you have a point?"

Her snottiness irritated me, and that sharpened my senses a little. "My point is, Tessa needs help figuring out what's going on. I'm planning to do what I can, and I thought you might want to . . . you know . . . join in."

Deirdre laughed out loud, her expression incredulous. "Am I hearing things?" she exclaimed. "The famous Nancy Drew wants me to join her little mystery club? Ooh, can I learn the secret handshake, too, or do I have to wait for my secret decoder ring to arrive first?"

I frowned, annoyed by her sarcasm. For a moment I was tempted to drop the whole thing. But the memory of Tessa's anxious face kept me going.

"Listen," I said sharply, "I know you're not exactly my biggest fan." I took a deep breath, stopping short of pointing out that the feeling was completely mutual. "But this time you should be able to see that we're both on the same side here. If word gets out that things are going wrong here at the spa, it could be a public relations disaster for Tessa. Her business could be ruined. She might have to shut down."

Deirdre's eyes widened slightly. I could see that I'd scored a point. She didn't want the fancy new spa run out of town any more than I did, though only for her own selfish reasons.

"They wouldn't shut down just because of one stupid little temperature malfunction," Deirdre said, though she didn't sound quite as confident as usual.

"Probably true," I agreed. Despite the seriousness of the situation, I couldn't help feeling slightly amused that Deirdre's life-threatening moment of terror had suddenly changed into a "stupid little temperature malfunction." "But that's not the only thing that's happened," I added.

As I quickly filled her in on the mystery meat in the chili, I heard footsteps hurrying toward us from farther down the hall. It was Bess.

"Marletta finally got bored with the kitchen and went to check out the dining room," she reported breathlessly. She glanced cautiously at Deirdre. "Everything okay here?"

I nodded. "Deirdre and I were just . . . discussing the case."

"Yeah, and I guess I might be willing to help," Deirdre added, glancing at me. "I definitely don't want this place to go under. And you guys will never be able to dig out the real scoop like I can. I mean, you don't even know half the people who are here today." As she spoke, her tone shifted from begrudging to self-satisfied.

Meanwhile Bess's jaw had dropped open, making her look a little like a fish gasping for air. I shot her a warning glance.

If Deirdre noticed Bess's shock, she didn't let on. "But it had better not get in the way of my turn in the mud bath. I'm on the schedule for two o'clock." She glanced at the clock on the table beneath the mirror. "That reminds me—I've got an aromatherapy session in, like, five minutes."

"I'll walk you there," I said, falling into step as Deirdre headed down the hall. Bess followed, still looking stunned. "We should probably figure out what kinds of questions you'll ask people to find out if they know anything."

"Don't bother." Deirdre waved one hand impatiently. "I know how to find out what's going on. Just leave it to me."

I bit my lip, wanting to argue, but I knew better than to push it too much. Otherwise she might change her mind about joining the investigation. And as much as I hated to admit it, I really could use her help on this one.

"All right," I said reluctantly. We turned a corner and saw the entrance to the aromatherapy suite just ahead. "We'll catch up with you later, then, I guess."

"Whatever." Without another word Deirdre disappeared through the door.

"Okay. What was *that* all about?" Bess demanded.

I sighed. "I'll explain in a sec," I promised. "First I want to check on something."

I had just noticed that we were down the hall from the lobby. Even though Tessa had assured me that her ex-husband hadn't tried to enter the spa, I figured it wouldn't hurt to double-check that information with the receptionist.

After the dim, pinkish, relaxing lighting of the interior halls, the natural sunlight pouring through the floor-to-ceiling windows in the large, airy lobby seemed brighter than ever. Bess and I stepped toward the main desk, and I saw that there was still a line of people waiting to get inside, though it was much shorter than it had been earlier that morning. A pair of efficient, elegantly dressed receptionists were hard at work checking people in and answering questions. I drifted to a spot at the edge of the desk, waiting for the right moment to interrupt.

Finally one of the receptionists noticed and turned toward me with a smile. "Hello, ladies," she said with a polite smile. "Can I help with someth—"

The rest of her query was lost in a sudden, crashing blast of noise as one of the huge lobby windows exploded into a million shards of glass.

6

A Questionable Suspect

Bess let out a loud shriek, and I instinctively ducked down behind the desk. A few moments of chaos followed. Peeking over the edge of the desk, I saw people running this way and that, most of them not seeming to know which way to go to escape.

"Wh-what was that?" Bess whimpered from behind me.

"I'm not sure," I said, still peering out at the shattered window. "I think maybe someone threw something at the window from outside."

I stood up and stepped out from my hiding place. "Wait!" Bess said. "What if it happens again?"

"I doubt it will," I said, staring intently toward the window.

I was vaguely aware that the receptionist was paging

Tessa, her voice shaking slightly. But I was more interested in what was going on outside. I watched as several police officers wrestled someone to the ground. I winced when I recognized that someone as Thomas Rackham.

"What's happening? Are we under attack?" an older woman was shouting loudly from somewhere nearby.

"Please calm down, madam," the second receptionist was urging frantically. "Someone just threw something at the window, that's all, and it's being taken care of."

I saw that she was right. A dark, solid-looking object was lying in the mess of broken glass just inside the window. It was about the size of a grapefruit, and for a moment I thought it was just a rock.

Then I stepped a little closer, picking my way carefully through the sharp-edged shards for a better look.

"What is it?" Bess asked from behind me. She might be a girly-girl, but she's no chicken. As soon as she'd spotted the police at work, she had come out of hiding and followed me across the lobby.

"I'm not sure." I pulled my sleeve down over my hand as I bent to pick up the object, even though I suspected the police wouldn't need to dust for fingerprints to know who had thrown it. I assumed they'd been keeping a careful watch on Thomas and his cronies all morning. If he was the one who'd tossed it, there should be no shortage of eyewitnesses.

A closer look revealed that the rocklike item was actually a crude stone carving of a turtle. "There's something written on the shell," I told Bess, squinting to read the words, which appeared to be scrawled in red permanent marker. "It says, 'Habitat theft, the killer Indulgences.'"

I glanced out at Thomas Rackham. The police had him in handcuffs now. I realized I'd barely thought about him and his protest since seeing him earlier. Could he be the one behind all the trouble? He seemed to have motive enough—he wanted to see the spa shut down.

Realizing that I'd have to hurry if I wanted to talk to him before the police dragged him away, I hurried toward the door. Behind me I heard Tessa's voice, and she sounded very upset. But I didn't hang around to see her reaction—I could talk to her later. Instead I continued on my way outside, making a beeline for Thomas Rackham Jr.

As I approached, one of the police officers surrounding Thomas glanced up. I saw that it was Chief McGinnis, the head of the River Heights PD.

"Why, it's Nancy Drew," he said sarcastically. "Fancy meeting you here, Nancy. Nice outfit."

I smiled weakly, glancing down at my robe and

slippers. For some reason the chief seems to think that I'm a magnet for trouble. Or maybe he thinks the *trouble* is the magnet, and I'm drawn to it. I'm not quite sure, since he tends to get a little incoherent when he's talking about it. Bess and George think it's because I sometimes—completely unintentionally of course—make him look bad by solving crimes before he does. It's probably a good thing Chief McGinnis likes and respects my father so much, or he'd probably have an even lower tolerance for my amateur sleuthing than he already does.

"Hi, Chief McGinnis," I said politely, deciding it might be wise to deliberately misunderstand his comment. "Of course I'm here—practically the whole town is here for the big grand opening!"

The chief responded with a disgruntled snort. "Well, stand back," he said. "We're going to be taking this vandal away in a moment."

"Hey, Nancy," Thomas greeted me, his eyes shining with excitement. "Looks like I will be calling your dad soon, after all."

I sighed. "Thomas, that wasn't a very smart thing to do," I chided him gently. "I know you're upset about the turtle thing, but—"

"Someone has to speak for the turtles!" Thomas cried passionately, struggling briefly against his handcuffs. "They have no voice with which to cry! I had to do it—that rock was my wake-up call for the uncaring antiturtle establishment!"

Maybe this mystery was going to be easier to solve than I'd expected.

"What about the meat in the chili?" I said. "How'd you manage that one, Thomas?"

"Meat?" Thomas repeated blankly. "I never eat meat. Meat is murder!"

I blinked. "Wait," I said. "Are you telling me you didn't have anything to do with the chili?"

Thomas shrugged. "What are you talking about?"

The chief was staring at me too. "Yes, Nancy," he said. "What *are* you talking about?"

"Wait," I said, my mind spinning. "Thomas, you admit to throwing that turtle rock through the window just now, right?"

"Of course!" Thomas tipped his unshaven chin up proudly. "I'm not afraid to take action on behalf of my silent, shelled friends of the earth."

"But you don't know anything about who put meat in the chili or messed with the sauna?" I urged.

Thomas wrinkled his nose. "Sauna?" he said. "Nancy, there's no time for sitting around in a sauna when there are turtles to be saved. Even if the sauna weren't inside a spa of death." He gestured dramatically toward the spa—well, as dramatically as he could, considering the handcuffs.

"Nancy, I think you'd better explain what—just a moment." The chief's walkie-talkie radio was buzzing. He spoke quietly into it for a moment, then switched it off and glanced at the other two officers holding on to Thomas. "Be right back. Just hold him here for now."

"Sure thing, Chief," one of the other officers said as Chief McGinnis turned and hurried off toward the squad car.

I decided I'd better make myself scarce before the chief returned and continued his interrogation. It wasn't that I wanted to withhold information from the police exactly. I just didn't think it was my place to tell them about everything that had happened. After all, none of it could be definitely ruled a crime at this point. If Tessa wanted the police to investigate, she ought to be the one to involve them.

Besides, it was starting to seem pretty clear that Thomas wasn't behind the chili and sauna problems, which meant that the window incident might just be unconnected to the rest of the sabotage. Or was it . . . ?

On a hunch I stuck around just long enough to ask Thomas one more question. "Thomas," I said, "how did you get so interested in these particular turtles, anyway?"

"Someone sent an e-mail alert about it to my Web site," Thomas said.

"Someone?" I said.

He shrugged. "Don't know who," he said. "It was an unknown return address, and it wasn't signed. But the important thing was, the info in the e-mail all checked out. I double-checked the links myself, and it's all true. This used to be a turtle habitat back before River Heights got so big."

Just then there was a shout from nearby. Chief McGinnis was standing near the curb, waving at the officers holding Thomas.

"That's our cue," one of the officers said, taking a firmer grip on Thomas's arm. "Come on, buddy. Let's get moving."

"Keep the faith, Nancy," Thomas called as the officers steered him toward the squad car. "And tell your dad I'll be calling soon!"

"Will do." I stepped back to let them pass, thinking about what Thomas had just told me. It seemed a little strange that his whole protest had arisen out of what basically amounted to an anonymous tip. What did that mean? Did it mean anything at all, or was I just muddying the issue by trying to make Thomas's presence into part of the mystery instead of a separate issue?

As I glanced around for Bess I was just in time to see Marletta and her little entourage rushing out of the lobby. "Excuse me!" the reporter shouted after the police officers, rushing toward the squad car with her robe flapping behind her. "Channel RH News! Excuse me!"

The police didn't respond, brushing off Marletta's questions as they herded Thomas into the car and drove off. Marletta just stood there for a moment, looking vexed. Then her assistant, Lulu, tugged on her sleeve and pointed to the other protesters. Ever since Thomas's arrest, they'd been milling around rather aimlessly on the sidewalk near the spa.

Marletta's face lit up. Gesturing for the cameraman to follow, she strode toward the protesters. But they were already starting to disperse, looking rather sheepish. One young woman stopped to talk to the reporter, though I couldn't hear what she was saying. Meanwhile the rest disappeared into the park or wandered off down the street. One college-age young man even turned his TURTLE POWER sign over, revealing another message on the other side that read BUGS ARE PEOPLE TOO. He headed across the street and took up a new position in front of the Pampered Pooch.

"Hey," Bess said, appearing beside me. "What's going on out here?"

I glanced over at her. "I was just watching poor Marletta's story disappear in front of her eyes," I said with a rueful chuckle. I told her what had happened with Thomas, finishing by pointing out the lone pro-tester in front of the pet store.

Bess squinted at the guy's new sign. "Bugs are people too?" she said. "What does that mean? Is he protesting that the store sells flea collars or some-thing?"

I grinned. "Could be," I said. "But my guess is that he's against those feeder bugs and stuff. Haven't you ever seen Bug Alley?"

Bess shook her head. "I'm almost afraid to ask. . . ."

"It's at the back of the store," I said. "It's where they sell feeder crickets and worms and stuff that people feed to their reptiles and things. They also have a few tarantulas and other exotic creepy crawlies. They like to brag that they're the only store in the tri-county area that sells those giant hissing cockroaches."

"Ugh." Bess shuddered. "Sounds lovely."

Just then I noticed Marletta's interview subject hurrying past us. Glancing over, I saw that the reporter was once again standing with microphone in hand, looking dejected.

"Oh, well," she said to her companions. "Guess we might as well head back inside."

"What about that guy?" Lulu pointed to the pet-store protester. "You could still get a quote from him."

Marletta glanced across the street and shrugged.

"I guess," she said, not sounding very hopeful.

"Go ahead!" Lulu said encouragingly. "Go on, Mike. Get some establishing shots of the pet shop." She poked the cameraman in the arm, and he obligingly raised the camera to his shoulder.

As Marletta headed across the street, I glanced back at the spa. If she was going to be busy outside for a few more minutes, it might be the perfect time to do some investigating without worrying about her turning up with her camera at a bad time.

"Come on," I told Bess. "Let's go in and check out the kitchen again. I want to see if I missed any clues."

The two of us headed back into the lobby. Several spa employees were already there with brooms and dustpans cleaning up the broken glass, while Tessa supervised a handyman who was carefully removing the remaining broken glass from the window pane.

I was about to go over to talk to Tessa when I thought I heard someone whispering my name. Glancing around, I saw Deirdre gesturing to me furiously from the door leading back into the spa.

"Nancy, over here!" Deirdre called.

Bess and I exchanged a glance. "Be right back," I said. "This shouldn't take long."

I walked over to Deirdre, leaving Bess to wander over toward Tessa. Deirdre grabbed me by the arm and yanked me through the door into the hallway beyond. Then she pulled me around the corner to a private spot.

"Where in the world have you been?" Deirdre snapped when the two of us were alone. "I've been looking all over for you! I mean, what kind of detective disappears right in the middle of an investigation?"

I opened my mouth to explain where I'd been, then closed it again. It just wasn't worth it.

"Sorry," I said instead, smiling to disguise my sudden desire to smack her. "What's up? Did you find out something interesting?"

Deirdre's irritated expression was replaced by a pleased smirk. "Better than that," she said proudly. "I cracked this case wide open!"

"Really?" I said, trying to hide my skepticism. "What do you mean?"

"I was just in the juice bar with Mrs. O'Malley and Mrs. Wright—you know them, of course? From the country club?" Deirdre said. "Well, we were just chatting about this and that. The new water hazard on the golf course, the library fund-raiser . . ."

"Yes?" I said with a touch of impatience. "And?"

Deirdre shrugged. "And they shared a juicy little bit of gossip," she said. "Apparently one of the spa's employees was fired right before the grand opening— seems Tessa Monroe caught her letting her six-year-old make mud pies in the mud room after hours."

"Yes?" I repeated, wishing that Deirdre would just get to the point. "So what?"

"So this." Deirdre leaned closer, looking very self-satisfied. "The ex-employee used to clean the Wrights' pool, so Mrs. Wright knows her. And she saw her here today . . . posing as a customer!"

7

Confusing Clues

Judging by Deirdre's self-satisfied smirk, she seemed to think that she'd dropped a bombshell, but I found myself underwhelmed by the impact of her information. "Okay," I said slowly. "So you think this person might be behind all the sabotage?"

"Of course!" Deirdre said in a tone that indicated she thought I might be a little slow. "You're supposed to be the great detective—don't you get it? This woman is trying to get back at Tessa for firing her!"

"Well, I suppose that's possible," I said. "It seems a little far-fetched, though." Still, I couldn't help remembering that Patsy, the chef, had told me a similar story about someone being fired. Was it the same person? I remembered that Patsy had mentioned something about her person being fired over a turkey sandwich, but she'd also mentioned that the employee had been in trouble for other things. Whether or not it was the same person, was getting fired enough of a motive for someone to sabotage the spa?

Suddenly I noticed Deirdre staring over my shoulder with a sour expression. "Are you still here?" she said. "I thought you must have left to play computer games or something by now."

Glancing behind me, I saw George hurrying toward us. I raised an eyebrow, realizing it was the first time I'd seen her since her abrupt departure from the kitchen doorway earlier. I wasn't even sure if she knew about everything that had been happening.

"Where have you been?" I asked her.

"Never mind," George said breathlessly. "I think you'd better get back to the lobby, Nancy."

"Why? Did Bess send you?" I wondered if Bess had found out something important from talking to Tessa.

George shook her head. "Just come on," she said darkly. "Something weird is happening out there."

I shrugged and followed. When I stepped into the lobby, I saw that the spa employees were still cleaning up the broken glass. Bess was there too, holding a dustpan for one of the workers. Nearby, Tessa was talking with two plump, pleasant-looking older women wearing pink aprons.

I blinked in surprise. "Hey, aren't those the ladies from Head to Toe?" I said, recognizing them from the TV coverage the night before.

"Yup," George said grimly. "Pretty coincidental for them to stop by right now, don't you think?"

Deirdre cocked an eyebrow. "You think those two old biddies have something to do with all the sabotage stuff?" she said. "No way. Besides, I was just telling Nancy, I already solved the mystery."

George rolled her eyes. "Yeah, right," she said sarcastically. "That'll be the day, when *you* tell Nancy how to solve a mystery!"

"Shut up, *Georgia*," Deirdre began hotly. "For your information, I—"

"Hey, Deirdre!" I interrupted, hoping to hush both of them before they really got rolling. "Um, why don't you go tell Bess what you found out? I'm sure she'll be interested."

I was also pretty sure Bess *might* forgive me for sticking her with Deirdre. Someday. But at the moment I just wanted Deirdre away from George before I had one more problem on my hands.

Once Deirdre wandered off, I glanced at George. "So you know about the sabotage?" I asked.

"Of course." George shrugged. "Bess just filled me in."

"Good." I hesitated, wanting to ask her where she'd

been all this time. But I decided there would be time enough for that later. Right now I wanted to make sure I didn't miss anything important while the scene of the crime was still fresh. Even though Thomas had confessed to the vandalism of the window, I couldn't totally shake the nagging suspicion that it was somehow connected to the other problems at the spa.

George and I stepped over toward Tessa. She was looking distraught as she split her attention between her busy employees and the two Head to Toe women.

"Wonder what they're doing here," George muttered suspiciously.

"Keep quiet, and maybe we'll hear!" I whispered.

We stood silently for a moment, pretending to watch the cleanup. From what I could hear, the two older women seemed to be alternating between congratulating Tessa on her grand opening and cooing over the broken window. Tessa's smile looked a little strained as she murmured her thanks for their kindness and concern.

Just then the lobby door swung open. I glanced over and saw another employee hurrying in, carrying a measuring tape.

"I'm sorry, ladies. Could you please excuse me a moment?" Tessa asked the two women. Then she waved at the new arrival. "Gloria, over here!" She hurried toward the employee.

I glanced at the Head to Toe ladies, who were watching as Tessa and Gloria headed for the broken window with the measuring tape. "I wonder if I should try to—"

I was startled when George suddenly took off in the middle of my sentence. Without a backward glance she disappeared through the door into the hall.

A moment later Bess wandered over, brushing off her hands on her robe. "Where was she going in such a hurry?" she asked, staring off in the direction George had gone.

I shrugged. "You got me," I said blankly. As if the mystery of the spa sabotage wasn't enough, it seemed that George was still acting like a nut. Speaking of nuts . . . "Where's Deirdre?"

"Got bored. Went to get her nails redone," Bess replied.

The Head to Toe ladies were still hovering over near the reception desk. Even though I doubted they had anything to do with the sabotage, I figured I might as well talk to them. Stranger people than they were had turned out to be guilty of bizarre things, and I'd learned never to assume anything about anybody.

"Excuse me," I said politely, stepping toward them. "Aren't you the owners of Head to Toe? My name is

Nancy Drew. I think you might know my house-keeper, Hannah Gruen?"

"Oh, yes!" The shorter of the two women beamed. "Hannah is just lovely! So you're young Nancy, are you?"

"We've read all about your adventures in the papers, my dear," the other woman added eagerly. "Such a clever girl you are, figuring out all those mysteries!"

"Thank you," I said, trying to ignore Bess's amused smirk. "I just wish I could figure out why someone would want to break the lobby window."

"Isn't it something?" the shorter woman said. "Poor dear Tessa is being so brave, but she must be beside herself. Why, I don't know what Marge and I would have done if we'd ever had such a thing happen over at our place."

The other woman nodded. "Of course, we don't have such lovely big windows there," she said contentedly. "Our salon is just the front wing of an old house, after all. But we love it there just the same."

"That's nice." I smiled politely. "Were you here when the window got broken?"

"Oh, no." Marge shook her head. "We missed all the excitement. We just arrived a moment ago and found out what had happened."

Her partner shook her head. "Such bad luck for poor dear Tessa," she murmured. She checked her watch. "Oh, dear. Sorry to be rude, Nancy, but I'm afraid we have to be going."

Marge gasped. "Oh, yes!" she exclaimed, glancing at her own watch. "Why, Ms. Waters will be arriving at any moment for her wash and trim. I do hope you'll excuse us, girls."

"Of course," Bess and I said in unison.

We watched as the pair rushed over to say goodbye to Tessa. A moment later they were gone.

"Well, George may think those two are suspicious," I said. "But Bess, somehow I can't picture them being involved in the sabotage." I shrugged and sighed. "I suppose if it comes to it, we could check with their customers, see if they have an alibi for the times when the other stuff happened. But honestly, it hardly seems worth the effort at this point."

Bess nodded. "So what do we do next?"

"I'm not sure," I said as we started down the hall. "First let's see if we can find—"

"Hey, guys," George said, popping out of the doorway we were passing. "There you are."

"There *we* are?" I said in disbelief. "There *you* are. Where did you rush off to in such a hurry?"

George shrugged. "Did it look like I was in a hurry?" she said casually. "I just decided it was a good time to hit the restroom."

"Oh." I gazed at her for a moment, wondering if

perhaps she wasn't feeling well. That might explain the unusual grumpiness of the past couple of days, not to mention the sudden bathroom breaks.

Once again I pushed George's weirdness out of my mind. That mystery could wait a little longer. I wanted to get to the bottom of Tessa's problems before word of the sabotage got out—or the saboteur struck again.

"This case is starting to get complicated," I told my friends. "I think we need to sit down and go over . . ."

I paused as a gaggle of women rounded the corner, all wearing Indulgences robes. They were chattering excitedly about the mud room and hardly seemed to notice our presence. Still, I waited until they had disappeared into the ladies' room before continuing.

"I think we need to find somewhere private to talk," I said. "I don't want any of the other customers to overhear. Where should we go?"

Bess smiled. "I have an idea," she said. "Follow me."

A few minutes later the three of us were stepping into one of the spa's semiprivate steam rooms, wrapped in fluffy white towels. We took our seats on the slatted wooden benches, leaning back to let the warm, moist air envelop us.

"Okay," I began briskly. "Let's start out by going

over what's happened. We have the meat appearing in the chili while Patsy was out of the room—"

"Unless Patsy was lying and put it there herself," Bess pointed out.

I smiled. My friends have learned a lot from hanging around with me and my dad over the years. "I thought of that too," I agreed. "But we'll come back to suspects in a second. We also have Deirdre's experience in one of these." I gestured to our steam room.

George shrugged, pushing back her short hair, which was already damp from the steam. "Yeah," she said. "*If* we believe that really happened, and it wasn't just Deirdre looking for attention by making up stories."

"Right," I said. "And finally we have the lobby window. That's three incidents. All took place within a fairly short period of time, and all of them could make Tessa look bad."

Bess stretched out one leg and propped it on the bench across from her. "True," she agreed. "So what are our clues? There's the turtle-shaped rock. . . ."

"Right," I said. "And that clump of blond hair I found in the kitchen—I'm still not sure that's a real clue, but I think we should keep it in mind." I paused, realizing that was the only other real physical clue we had. "Okay. Am I forgetting anything?"

George sneezed. "I don't know," she said. "It's hard to think when you're sitting around, cooking in steam like a bunch of broccoli."

I ignored her. "Okay, now the suspect list," I said. "*That* seems to be growing by the moment. I still think Tessa's ex-husband, Dan, is near the top of the list."

"Tessa didn't seem to think he'd really do anything, though," Bess pointed out, dabbing at her forehead with the corner of her towel. "Besides, she said that if he tried to come into the spa, her employees would let her know, remember?"

I nodded. "But they could only do that if they actually saw him," I pointed out. "It's not like there's an armed guard at every door in this place. He could have sneaked in through the back after their argument earlier. Or he could be working with someone on the inside—someone posing as a customer, or even one of the employees."

"But don't forget Thomas Rackham," George said. "The police actually saw him break the window. He seems like the natural top suspect. Plus he definitely has a motive—he wants this place shut down."

"I know," I replied thoughtfully. "But I just don't believe he's responsible for the other pranks. The meat thing, maybe—though I'm not sure a true-blue vegetarian would buy or handle meat even to make a point."

Bess squinted. "Yeah, that's true if you're talking about someone like Tessa or Patsy or Marletta," she pointed out. "But Thomas is the type that will do anything to get attention."

"Just about anything," I said. "But Thomas has always seemed basically harmless, you know? And the stunt with the steam room was awfully dangerous. What if there had been some elderly person in there relaxing instead of Deirdre? That could have been deadly. I just don't see Thomas pulling something like that."

"Okay," George said. "So who else might want to cause trouble for the spa?"

"Well, there's Deirdre's theory." I filled them in on Deirdre's story about the disgruntled ex-employee, as well as Patsy's mention of a similar situation earlier. "I don't know if it's the same person, or even if Deirdre's gossip is true," I finished. "But it's probably worth checking out."

"If you ask me, *Deirdre* is worth checking out," George said. "I still wouldn't be surprised if she rigged the whole sauna thing herself."

"I suppose that's possible," I said diplomatically, wiping a bit of condensation off my chin with one hand. "But she couldn't have done the meat thing too. That would have meant being in two places at once."

"What about the Head to Toe ladies?" Bess asked.

"Better keep them on the list too," I said. "They seem so sweet, I can't believe they'd be so underhanded. Then again, they're the ones who might lose a lot of business if Indulgences is a hit. And money is a strong motive for people to commit crimes."

George shrugged. "So is revenge."

"I know," I agreed. "That's why I want to find out more about Dan Monroe and this mysterious ex-employee." I glanced over at Bess. Her cheeks had taken on an even rosier glow than usual in the moist heat. "Feel like doing a little snooping?"

"Sure," Bess said. "Just so we make sure to leave enough time to grab some lunch before our appointment in the mud room. All this pampering is making me really hungry."

"Don't worry," I said, checking the clock set into the instrument panel on the steam room wall. "We've still got plenty of time for all that."

Bess nodded agreeably. "So what do you want me to do?"

"Go see if the police are still outside," I said. "Talk to them a little, or anyone else who's out there. Just generally snoop around and see if you can figure out if Dan Monroe is still hanging around. And of course, if you do find Dan, chat with him and see what you can find out."

I knew this kind of assignment was right up Bess's alley. With her natural charm she would be able to convince people to tell her whatever they knew. Even the police would be less suspicious of her questions than they would be of mine.

"Okay," Bess said. "What are you guys going to be doing?"

"I think I'll go find Tessa, see if she has any ideas who might be behind this," I said. I glanced over at George. "How about if you try to figure out who this mysterious ex-employee is? You could start by asking around in the kitchen. For some reason Patsy's description made me think that's where she worked."

To my surprise, George scowled. "No way," she said abruptly.

I blinked. Bess turned to stare at her cousin in surprise.

"Huh?" I said, wondering if I'd misunderstood George's response somehow. "What's the matter?"

"Nothing!" George snapped, her voice suddenly angry. "Just forget it, all right? I'll go check out the stupid ex-husband thing if you want, but if you want someone to snoop around the tofu factory, you guys will have to do that yourself!"

Without another word, she jumped to her feet and stomped out of the steam room, slamming the door behind her.

8

A Juicy Secret

For a moment Bess and I just stared at each other in shock. Finally I found my voice.

"What was that all about?" I exclaimed.

Bess bit her lip. "I don't know," she said. "I mean, she's been acting kind of weird all day. . . ."

I nodded, realizing for the first time just how true that was. I'd been trying so hard to focus on the mysterious happenings at the spa, but really, George's behavior was very unusual—and worth some investigation of its own.

"You're right," I said. "I wonder if we should go try to find her and figure out what's wrong."

"Do you think she'd tell us?" Bess asked doubtfully. "She didn't seem exactly wanting to share just now."

I frowned. "What could be bothering her so much that we wouldn't already know about?"

"I don't know," Bess replied. "Last night I figured it was just the usual—lack of positive cash flow. We already know that can make her grumpy. But she never lets it bother her *this* much."

"Besides, this day at the spa is all free thanks to Dad's passes," I pointed out. "Getting free stuff usually puts her in a great mood."

"Good point," Bess said. She frowned. "But what else could it be?"

We tried to think of other possibilities for George's bad mood as we stepped out of the steam room into the attached dressing room, where our robes were waiting for us. I was just slipping on my robe when the door suddenly swung open.

"Do you mind?" Bess shrieked, quickly pulling her robe shut. "Oh, it's you."

I glanced over and saw Deirdre in the doorway. She ignored Bess and stepped toward me. "Listen," she said eagerly. "I just found out some more important information."

By the glint in her eyes, I guessed that "important information" translated to "juicy gossip." Still, that didn't mean it might not be useful to the case.

"What is it?" I asked her.

Deirdre leaned against the lockers in the small

dressing room. "I was just in the dining room talking to some of the ladies from the country club," she said. "Do you guys know Mrs. Ruthann Lundy?"

"Yes," I replied, trying hard not to add the word *unfortunately.* Mrs. Lundy is a loud, pushy, rather abrasive woman who's married to the most aggressive attorney in River Heights. Dad always says that Jackson Lundy would try to sue anything that isn't nailed down and half the stuff that is. He's known Lundy for years and has faced him in court a few times, and has several colorful nicknames for him that reflect his ambulance-chasing ways.

"Well, Mrs. Lundy was in the dining room too," Deirdre continued. "She was griping and complaining because she had to wait fifteen minutes for her bowl of vegetarian chili. She was so worked up about it that she actually insisted the waitress call Tessa to come and speak to her."

"Did she come?" Bess asked.

Deirdre nodded. "Mrs. Lundy layed into her for a while, and then she got even more upset because Tessa wouldn't let her jump to the front of the line at the mud bath. Said it wouldn't be fair to the other customers, and yadda yadda." She rolled her eyes. "I'll tell you, ol' Ruthann was *not* happy to hear that. She stormed out of the dining room yelling at the top of her lungs that she was going to put the spa out of business!"

I winced. The top of Ruthann Lundy's lungs was a scary thought indeed. Then I sighed, realizing I might have yet another suspect for the list. "Do you know how long Mrs. Lundy had been at the spa?" I asked Deirdre. "I mean, was she here all morning or did she just arrive in time for lunch?"

"What do I look like, her keeper?" Deirdre replied with a shrug. "I'm just telling you what I heard." She checked her watch. "Oops! Gotta go. Finally, almost time for my mud bath. But I want to have my pores clarified first."

She disappeared back out the door. I glanced over at Bess. "Okay, that was actually interesting," she said. "Do you think there's anything to it?"

"I don't know." I bit my lip, thinking about what Deirdre had said. "I suppose it's possible that Mrs. Lundy is trying to drum up business for her husband. A high-profile lawsuit could bring him a lot of publicity—and more clients. It's a little far-fetched but, knowing the Lundys, not impossible to believe."

"True," Bess agreed. "Remember how Lundy tried to sue that Seeing Eye dog for seventy-five million dollars or so? And then ran all those radio ads about it and everything? That got people talking for weeks. I'm sure he'd be up for something like suing the spa, especially since it's been in the news so much lately."

I sighed. "Good point," I said. "Guess maybe we should look into this angle a little more. Maybe I can track down some of Mrs. Lundy's friends and try to find out if they know anything."

"I'll help," Bess offered. "But I guess I should go cancel our aromatherapy session first. How about if I meet you in the dining room in about fifteen?"

"Sounds good. See you there."

We parted ways outside the steam room area, Bess hurrying toward the lobby while I headed for the dining room. As I rounded a corner in the hallway, I almost ran into Marletta Michaels's cameraman. He was crouching down as he filmed Marletta's feet, which were still encased in a pair of Indulgences slippers. Aside from the two of them, the hall was empty.

"Oops! Sorry," I said, veering out of the way just in time.

Marletta smiled at me. "Oh, hello there, Nancy," she said brightly. "Not your fault—we were just trying to get a few interesting establishing shots while we wait." She gestured to a door nearby. A sign on the door read FACIAL SUITE.

I returned her smile, a little surprised at the cheerful greeting. If she was holding a grudge against me for being a carnivore, she wasn't letting it show. I was also a bit surprised that she was still around. I wondered if she was planning to stay at the spa for the entire day.

"I see," I said. "So you're waiting your turn for a facial, hmm?"

I was just making small talk, preparing to move on. But Marletta responded with a broad grin.

"I suppose you could say that," she said meaningfully.

I had no idea what to make of her reaction. I was tempted to ignore it and move on, but that little sixth sense of mine was tingling all of a sudden. "I see," I said again, even though I really didn't—not yet. "Well, it certainly seems like you're having a nice time at the spa today."

"Oh, certainly!" Marletta said enthusiastically. "It's so nice that there's finally a true vegetarian/vegan haven here in River Heights. And having it be such a lovely facility is the tofu icing on the egg-free, dairy-free cake, so to speak." She winked at me. "But that's not the only reason I'm in a good mood," she added playfully. "See, I thought I was just here covering the grand opening. A nice little story, but not exactly Pulitzer material, you know?"

"Hmm," I said, not quite sure what she was driving at.

She smirked. "Oh, I shouldn't tell you." She glanced at her cameraman. "Mike, tell me to shut up before I spill the beans, would you?"

"Shut up, boss," Mike said obediently.

"I just can't!" Marletta trilled with laughter. "Anyway, I know the famous Nancy Drew would never give away my secret. . . ." After looking up and down the hall to make sure no one else was around, she leaned closer. Her carefully made-up eyes were sparkling with barely contained glee. "I just got a very interesting tip. Apparently there's a top-secret suite hidden somewhere in the spa building—and the First Lady of the United States is in there having her pores cleansed right now!"

9

Hair-Raising Suspicions

What?" **I blurted out** in alarm. I was quite certain that the First Lady was nowhere near River Heights at the moment, let alone right there in the spa. However, if Marletta started snooping around in pursuit of the ridiculous story, it made it all the more likely that she might uncover the real story at the spa that day— the sabotage.

Of course, the reporter already knew all about the Thomas Rackham incident. But that was really no biggie—nobody would think twice about another of Thomas's crazy stunts, no matter where it took place. No one would blame Tessa or the spa for that.

On the other hand, if word of the chili mistake and the steam room disaster were to get out, it could scare people off and ruin Tessa's business, or at least her reputation as a conscientious businesswoman. I couldn't let that happen. I needed to know what was really going on.

"Are—are you sure about your source?" I asked Marletta carefully. "I mean, the First Lady . . . It sounds a little, um . . ."

"That's why it's so *perfect*!" Marletta replied. "Nobody would expect her to spend time in a sleepy little place like River Heights. My guess is, it has something to do with Rackham Industries. You know how interested the First Lady is in charity work, and the company *does* donate a lot of money to all kinds of different charities. . . ."

"But why would she come to the spa?" I said. "It really doesn't make any—"

"Excuse me, Nancy," Marletta said eagerly, clearly not paying any attention at all to what I was saying. "I need to find Lulu and get her started on some quick research."

I sighed with frustration, realizing it was hopeless. Marletta was sure she was about to land the scoop of the century, and nothing I said was going to stop her from pursuing it. That meant she was going to be searching high and low through the spa until she tracked down the First Lady—or some other juicy story.

What a mess! The only way to fix things seemed

to be to wrap up the sabotage mystery quickly, before Marletta found out about it. As the reporter rushed off toward the lobby, I headed in the other direction in search of my friends. If I was going to solve this, I needed their help.

I found them both waiting for me in the restaurant. They'd been seated at a table behind a couple of potted palms, giving us a little privacy from the dozens of other diners who were there enjoying the spacious, well-appointed room. The restaurant ceiling was one big skylight, and the muted green walls and the large, healthy plants growing everywhere made the place feel like a beautiful glade.

"We already ordered for you," George told me as I sat down. "Food should be here soon."

"Good! I'm starving," I said, suddenly realizing it was true. "But listen—we've got to talk. For some reason Marletta thinks the First Lady of the U.S. is here at the spa. She's determined to track her down, which means she's more likely than ever to stumble across the real story."

Bess wrinkled her nose. "The First Lady? How would she get a crazy idea like that?"

"Maybe it's true," George suggested with a laugh.

I rolled my eyes. "I suppose anything's possible," I said.

But their comments made me think. Why *did*

Marletta think the First Lady was at the spa? I wished I'd asked her. It didn't make sense, and that made me wonder if it might have something to do with the sabotage. Was someone trying to encourage Marletta to snoop around?

"Anyway, we've really got to figure this problem out," I told my friends. "Let's go over that suspect list again, okay?"

Before we could do so, a waitress arrived with our lunch. Bess and George had ordered us each a bowl of the vegetarian chili, along with salads and drinks. Even without meat the chili still smelled great, and I dug in with enthusiasm. George looked a little skeptical at first, muttering something about tree huggers and tofu. But after her first, tentative spoonful, she seemed happy enough to slurp down the chili.

"Okay," Bess said once the waitress was gone. "So who are our suspects?"

I swallowed my bite of chili. "I'd still put Dan Monroe at the top of the list," I said. "We also can't really rule out Thomas Rackham, since we know he's responsible for at least part of the trouble. Then there are the ladies from Head to Toe, the mysterious ex-employee Deirdre and Patsy mentioned, and of course the Lundys—I still want to look into that one a little more." I paused, thinking. "Am I forgetting anyone? Who else might have a motive to mess up the grand opening?"

"What about Tessa herself?" George suggested. "Maybe she's trying to sabotage herself for some reason. I don't know what her motive would be, but she'd certainly have the opportunity to do all that stuff."

I thought about that for a moment. "I guess it's possible," I said. "She might want to make the business fail to collect insurance or something." I had to admit that it wasn't as far-fetched as some of the other possibilities, though I hated to think that the pleasant, likable owner could be behind all the trouble at her own spa.

Obviously Bess was troubled by that too. "Tessa?" she said doubtfully. "But she's so nice! Besides, there's not really any evidence pointing to her, is there?"

I sighed, playing with my spoon. "Unfortunately there's not much evidence pointing to *anyone* right now."

We talked it over a little more as we quickly finished our lunch. Then I pushed back my chair and stood up, feeling refreshed.

"I want to get a handle on some of these suspects," I told my friends. "Let's go find Deirdre."

We soon found her in the massage suite having her feet rubbed by a handsome young spa employee. She seemed less than pleased by our interruption.

"Make it fast, okay?" she said brusquely. "I'm due in the mud room in like forty-five minutes, my pores are open and ready, and I don't want to be late. Everyone is raving about that place. I can't believe I'm going to be practically the last person to get to try it today! It better be worth the wait."

I could tell that she was rapidly losing interest in playing detective. "This won't take much time, Deirdre," I said in as soothing a voice as I could muster. "You've just been so helpful today, and I was wondering if you might possibly remember anything else about that story you heard. You know, the one about that employee that got fired?"

Out of the corner of my eye I could see George rolling her eyes at my flattering tone. But Deirdre looked pleased.

"Well," she said, adjusting her robe as she leaned back in the massage chair. "I'll have to think. I seem to remember someone saying that—hey, Marco, I told you, concentrate on the arches!"

"Sorry, miss," the masseur said meekly, adjusting his grip on Deirdre's bare foot.

"That's better." Deirdre smiled, looking satisfied.

She glanced at me. "Oh, right. Let's see, I guess I forgot to tell you I remembered that girl's name."

"You mean the fired employee?" I said, surprised and excited. This could be a real break! "You know her name?"

Deirdre shrugged. "Sure," she said casually, as if surprised at my reaction. "Her name's Kaylene." She shuddered slightly. "She used to work at the country club before she got the job here. I totally remember her—she was, like, a walking fashion disaster. Ugly punked-out clothes, spiky blond hair, five-inch spikes, bad jewelry—the works. Luckily they made her slick down the hair at work and wear a uniform. But seeing her come in through the lobby all the time wasn't enjoyable. I don't know why the club doesn't have the employees come in through some kind of hidden back door or something. . . ."

I gritted my teeth. If Deirdre had all this extra information about one of our suspects, why hadn't she come to tell me? Still, I knew I shouldn't expect too much from her. It was lucky I was hearing it now!

"So she worked at the club," I prompted. "Why did she leave? Did she quit or get fired? Do you know her last name, or anything else about her?"

Deirdre glanced at me as Marco moved on to her other foot. "Geez, chill out with the questions, okay?" she said. "I feel like I'm on the stand. I think you're badly in need of a little relaxation—too bad your turn in the mud room isn't sooner."

"Deirdre," I said, trying as hard as I could to remain patient. "Please. This is important. I need to know anything you found out about this Kaylene person, okay?"

She shrugged. "Whatever," she drawled. "I don't remember too much about her from the club. But I know she got in trouble once for bringing her daughter to work with her when her baby-sitter didn't show. Oh, and I remember Daddy talking about her after she got fired. He said she kept threatening to sue for, like, wrongful terms or something."

"Wrongful *termination*," I corrected automatically, surprised as always that a fellow lawyer's daughter could be so ignorant of her father's work. I exchanged a meaningful glance with Bess and George. Now *this* was information that might be useful!

"I can describe what she looks like if you want," Deirdre offered. "Especially that horrible hairdo. I think it's still burned on my retinas. Ugh! What a waste of decent blond hair. Marco! Is that what *you* call an arch? Because I'm no anatomist, but I'm pretty sure it's a toe. . . ."

I took advantage of her distraction to mutter a quick good-bye and duck out of the room, followed by my friends. "Well," I said once we were out in the hall, "I guess it's time to start asking around about Kaylene."

Bess nodded. "I hate to admit it, but Deirdre is being useful for once."

"*If* what she said is true," George added. "Let's not forget the source here. Deirdre isn't exactly famous for her accuracy when it comes to information."

"Good point," I said. "But I still think we should check this out. Come on, let's start in the kitchen."

"The kitchen?" George said. "Why there?"

"Based on what Patsy said earlier, I think that's where the fired employee worked," I said. "Come on!"

Bess nodded, but George bit her lip. "I'll join you in a minute," she muttered quickly. "Er—I think I'll stop off in the bathroom first. . . ."

Without waiting for an answer, she spun and hurried off, disappearing around a corner. I blinked after her in surprise, but shook it off. I just couldn't waste any time trying to figure out my friend's weird behavior right now.

"What Deirdre just told us puts a whole new spin

on things," I commented as Bess and I hurried down the hall. "It really sounds as if Kaylene could be the culprit."

Bess nodded. "It all sort of fits," she agreed. "She's familiar with the layout of the spa, since she worked here. And she knows the other employees—all it would take would be one friend here to sneak her in."

"And that blond hair I found fits," I said. I grinned. "Even if we doubt the rest of her gossip, I'm totally confident that Deirdre got Kaylene's hairdo description right." My smile faded as I thought about the case. "And now we know her motive might not be simple revenge," I added. "Deirdre said Kaylene threatened to sue the club for firing her. Maybe she's setting herself up for a lawsuit here, too. If she makes Tessa look like a careless person with all these 'accidents,' it'll make her own case seem that much stronger to a jury."

We cut our discussion short as we reached the kitchen door. When we pushed through it, I saw that it was much busier than it had been earlier—about a dozen employees were scurrying around in a sort of controlled chaos as they dished up lunch for the hungry patrons out in the restaurant. I spotted Patsy over near the chili pot; she appeared to be guarding the pot and ladling out every bowl personally. Even though I doubted the saboteur would strike twice in the same way, I couldn't really blame her.

I felt bad about bothering people when they were so busy, but I didn't have much choice. If news of the sabotage got out, their jobs could be in danger.

Bess and I split up and started asking the employees about Kaylene. It didn't take much to get people talking about her. Everyone I approached seemed downright eager to describe how lazy she had been, how unwilling to help others, and how quick to take offense. It seemed that even before the turkey sandwich incident—and the mud pie incident Deirdre had described, which several of the kitchen employees mentioned as well—Kaylene had hardly been a model employee.

After a few minutes Bess hurried over. "Wow," she murmured. "Are you hearing the kinds of stuff I'm hearing about this Kaylene character?"

I nodded, glancing around to make sure no one was near enough to overhear us. "She certainly seems unpopular around here," I muttered back. "But I'm not sure it's making our case any simpler. I mean, it's easy to believe such an unpleasant-sounding person would pull some of these sabotage stunts. But it also sounds like nobody here would cover up if they spotted her. And other than Deirdre's source, nobody has mentioned seeing her at the spa today." I sighed, shaking my head. "In fact, I'd be surprised if Kaylene dared to show her face anywhere near here today."

Bess gasped. She was staring at a point somewhere over my left shoulder. "Are you sure about that?" she exclaimed. "Because I think that's her!"

False Leads and New Clues

I spun around just in time to see a spiky-haired young woman disappearing into the dining room. "Come on!" I said, dashing after her with Bess at my heels.

We caught up to our quarry a few yards into the restaurant. She had paused to ogle a dessert tray sitting on a stand near the waiters' station.

"Excuse me," I blurted out. "Is your name Kaylene?"

The young woman glanced up, her wide blue eyes guileless and unconcerned. "No," she said pleasantly. "But you're pretty close. It's Kate."

"Kate?" I repeated. "But that's not your full name, right? It's Kaylene?"

"Not Kaylene." The young woman looked more perplexed than ever. "Kate. Just Kate."

After another moment or two of slightly confused conversation, I figured out that the young spiky-haired woman wasn't just being difficult. She wasn't the mysterious Kaylene at all—just another spa customer who happened to have a similar hairstyle. After apologizing for disturbing her, Bess and I wandered back toward the kitchen.

"Well, that was embarrassing," I muttered.

Bess nodded. "I'm sorry, I should have known," she said sheepishly. "Deirdre said Kaylene had five-inch spikes, remember? Kate's hair was only a couple of inches long. And it was more just gelled than actually spiked. . . ."

I nodded distractedly, less than interested in the intricate details of various hairstyles. All I cared about was that time was passing, and we weren't getting any closer to an answer. Plus my famous hunch-o-meter was starting to tell me that the whole Kaylene theory might be a false lead. I wondered if Mrs. Wright had mistaken Kate for Kaylene as Bess and I had, or if Deirdre's gossip had just gotten it wrong, as usual.

Flagging down a passing waitress who had spent several minutes earlier describing Kaylene's various indiscretions, I asked her one last question: "Does Kaylene still have spiky blond hair?"

The waitress looked bemused. "Oh, no way," she

replied. "Tessa warned her the first day that she wouldn't be able to wear it like that at work. So Kaylene went right out and got it changed." The waitress headed back into the kitchen and we followed.

"To what?" Bess asked. "You mean she got rid of the spikes?"

"Yeah. But that's not all." The waitress rolled her eyes. "Don't know if she wanted to spite Tessa, or just has horrible taste. But she had it dyed, like, magenta. And cut into a weird little pageboy."

I sighed. It shouldn't have been a huge surprise that Deirdre's big scoop had led me down the wrong path. But I couldn't help feeling discouraged. It seemed we were back at square one.

I thanked the waitress, and as she hurried off, Bess and I huddled in a corner of the kitchen. "Guess we can cross Kaylene off our suspect list," I commented.

"Are you sure?" Bess asked. "She still has a good motive."

"I know," I said. "But the more I talk to these people, the less I believe she'd be able to sneak in here and do so much damage without someone spotting her. Especially with hot pink hair." I glanced toward the chili pot across the busy kitchen. "Plus she couldn't be the one who left that blond hair near the stove earlier."

"Good point," Bess said. "So what's next?"

"Let's find George," I said. "We need to start looking into some of these other suspects, pronto."

But we were only a few steps down the hall outside the kitchen when we heard the sound of loud voices. We exchanged a glance as we both recognized Tessa's voice.

"Come on," I whispered, leading the way.

When we pushed our way through the door leading into the main hallway, we saw Tessa and Marletta facing off a few yards away. Marletta's cameraman was there too, though he wasn't taping at the moment.

". . . and I can assure you, there's no truth to those rumors!" Tessa was saying firmly, her normally calm face bright red as she glared at Marletta. "And if you don't stop harassing my employees while they're trying to work, I'll have to ask you to leave!"

"Come on, Tessa," Marletta retorted sharply. "You can't hide something like this forever."

For a split second my heart leaped into my throat as I thought Marletta had uncovered the sabotage. But Tessa's next words reassured me—at least slightly.

"I'm not hiding anything," Tessa said. "I swear to you, I've never even met the First Lady!"

I shuddered, partly with relief and partly with worry. It was clear from Marletta's expression that she wasn't backing down on the First Lady thing. But if I didn't figure out this case soon, things were only going to get crazier—especially if the saboteur decided to strike again, a possibility I was trying not to think about too much.

"Let's get out of here," I whispered to Bess, pulling her down the hall away from Tessa and Marletta. Neither woman seemed to have noticed us, though as we rounded the corner and I glanced over my shoulder, I saw the cameraman staring after us curiously.

We found George a few minutes later in one of the massage rooms. She was leaning against an empty massage table, humming along with the New Age music playing over the speakers and watching as a dark-skinned masseuse worked on a plump woman in her fifties. I recognized the woman as Mrs. Hancock, a member of the country club set and a friend of Mrs. Lundy's. It looked like she and George were having a conversation.

"Hi," I said, wondering what in the world George was doing hanging out with someone like Mrs. Hancock. "Sorry to interrupt."

"That's okay," George said. "Mrs. H here was just telling me all the latest gossip."

"Oh, don't be naughty, Georgia," Mrs. Hancock said complacently, glancing up from the massage table. "Don't listen to a thing she says, girls. We were just chatting about the most innocent things, really."

I was a little surprised at how chummy George and the older woman were acting until I remembered that Mrs. Hancock was a regular customer of George's mother's catering company. Then I saw George wink at me as Mrs. Hancock turned away briefly to speak to the masseuse.

"Mrs. H was just telling me how her friend Mrs. Lundy used to live next door to Tessa," George said calmly. "Isn't that right, Mrs. H?"

I smiled, realizing that George was just as hard at work on our case as Bess and I were. Then my smile faded slightly as I realized what she'd just said.

"Wait," I said. "Mrs. Hancock, is that true? Tessa and Mrs. Lundy are neighbors?"

"*Were* neighbors," Mrs. Hancock corrected, pushing herself up on her elbows to look at us as the masseuse went to work on the backs of her legs. "When Tessa was still married to Dan. Tessa and Ruthann were quite friendly—at least until Jackson agreed to represent Dan in the divorce."

My eyes widened, and I traded a glance with my friends. This was interesting news indeed, and cast a whole new light on the case, not to mention Mrs. Lundy's behavior. Could Ruthann Lundy and Dan Monroe be in cahoots? Would people like the Lundys really stoop to sabotage? This was all getting very complicated. . . .

Just then Mrs. Hancock's cell phone rang. She grabbed it from the nearby table. "Hello?" she trilled into it. "Oh, Ruthann, how are you? Are you at the club?"

Gesturing to my friends, I tiptoed away from the massage table.

"Well?" George murmured, looking pleased with herself. "Did I score, or what?"

"Possibly," I said.

George frowned. *"Possibly?"* she repeated. "Come on! This is totally big news, admit it."

"Sorry, you're right." I smiled at her. "Good work, George. I just don't know quite how it all fits with the other information we have. You know?"

Bess nodded. "The more we find out, the less it all makes sense," she whispered. "I know the Lundys are a little nutty, but I can't imagine them pulling something like this sabotage."

I nodded. My head was starting to ache, and the icky New Age music in the massage suite wasn't helping any. I shook my head, trying to clear it—or maybe shake the jumble of clues and information I'd gathered in my mind into some sort of sensible pattern. There was something tugging at the back of my mind, some tingling that was telling me I was missing some important connection or meaning.

Taking a deep breath, I glanced over at Mrs.

Hancock, who was still occupied with her phone call. Then I looked back at my friends.

"We need to stop for a minute," I said. "We've been bouncing around from one idea to another all day, and that's obviously not working. We need to get logical about this, look at the facts, or—"

"AAAAAAAAAAAAAAAAAAAH!"

We all jumped as an ear-piercing shriek erupted from somewhere just outside the suite. It was immediately followed by the sound of running feet.

"What was that?" Bess gasped.

I was already racing for the door, with George right behind me. "Let's find out!" I exclaimed.

We dashed out of the suite. Right outside was a small sitting area. On the far side of that was the door leading into the extravagant mud room. I hadn't been through that door yet, but several people had pointed it out at various times that day.

At the moment the door was standing open. More screams and shouts were coming from inside.

I hurried through the door and stopped short. For a second I was distracted by the room itself—in person it looked even larger and more impressive than it had on TV. Dozens of carved plaster columns supported an arched, soaring ceiling. Intricate mosaics and frescoes decorated every surface, giving the place a timeless elegance, while the lacy fronds of stately potted palms waved gently in the slight breeze of several large ceiling fans.

Then my attention turned to the small crowd gathered around the large mud tub in the center of the room. The screams and yells were coming from the group, which consisted mostly of customers wrapped in robes or towels, along with a couple of uniformed employees. Most of the customers were standing on the slatted teak benches or jumping up and down nearby. There was a sudden flurry of movement as several of them leaped aside with a new chorus of shrieks.

"What's going on?" Bess said as she joined me.

"I don't know," I murmured.

I took a step forward, craning my neck to get a better look at the mud tubs themselves. As I passed a large column and got a clear look at the largest tub, I immediately realized what everyone was so upset about.

Dozens of enormous cockroaches were scuttling out of the warm mud!

11

Bugging Out

"**G**ross!" **Bess squealed, jumping** backward as one of the large insects skittered in our direction and let out a menacing hiss. It was huge, easily three inches long. Its shiny blackish brown body gleamed in the sunlight pouring in through the skylights. There had to be at least two or three dozen of the ugly creatures in sight, scurrying across the paved floor, walking over the firm surface of the mud in several of the baths, even scurrying up the walls. The insects' hissing echoed off the tile walls and floors, making it sound like the place was filled with snakes. My jaw dropped in horror—not at the roaches, though they were large enough to make me look twice—but at the sight of Marletta staring eagerly at the scene. The reporter was standing in a different doorway, her entourage right behind her. The cameraman was already lifting his camera to his shoulder.

George noticed too. "Uh-oh," she murmured. "Tessa's not going to be able to cover up what's happening this time."

I gulped and nodded. The continuing screams were bringing everyone within earshot to the mud room. The doorways in each wall of the huge room were filling up with more spectators with every passing second, people craning their necks to get a better look.

Maybe this was my chance—my last chance?—to help Tessa figure out what was really going on. Glancing around, I quickly took note of who was already in the room. Whoever the saboteur was, he or she was probably still nearby, perhaps even in this very room!

I spotted Patsy, the head chef, huddled with several other kitchen employees in one doorway. "Quick," I whispered to Bess. "Which way is the kitchen from here?"

Bess blinked and tore her gaze away from the roaches long enough to answer me. "That way," she said, pointing toward the doorway at which I'd just been looking. "Why? Do you think the bugs came from there?"

I shook my head, grateful for Bess's unerring sense

of direction. Not only can she identify the shortest path between any two stores in the mall, but she almost always has a sense of north, south, east, and west.

Out of the corner of my eye I was vaguely aware that Marletta was walking toward the center of the room. She was moving slowly, so Lulu could quickly touch up the reporter's blond hair with a brush and a can of hairspray. I frowned, picturing the image of the giant roaches in the mud bath splashed all over the local TV news that evening. In a sleepy little city like River Heights, it was likely to be the lead story.

Feeling more desperate than ever, I continued my assessment of the room. Another doorway held one of the receptionists from the front desk, along with a smattering of other employees and customers.

I took a step forward, trying to figure out which spectators had just arrived and which might have been on the scene when the bugs appeared. Behind me I heard Bess gasp.

"Careful, Nancy," she said. "They're everywh—eeep!"

She jumped back as another cockroach scurried toward us, followed by a spa employee. I recognized the young man as Marco, the masseur we'd met earlier.

"Sorry, ladies," he said breathlessly, swooping toward the roach with an empty paper cup. He managed to capture it, sliding a piece of paper over the top of the cup to keep the insect contained. "We'll have these guys out of here in just a few minutes."

Without waiting for an answer, he hurried toward the door. I shuddered slightly. I'm not particularly squeamish about creepy crawlies, but I had to admit the roaches looked pretty nasty, especially close-up.

Based on the ongoing screams and cries, I could tell there were plenty of others who agreed. Glancing around again for the source of a particularly loud shriek, I spotted Deirdre standing along the wall of the room with a small group of her country club cronies. I gazed at her for a moment. In spite of everything, I had to admit that she had actually turned out to be sort of useful. If not for her, I might never have known about the whole Lundy situation, or known so much about Kaylene. Besides, it didn't hurt to have an extra pair of eyes on the lookout for anything suspicious.

I sighed, realizing that one extra set of eyes still might not be enough to solve this mystery. If only I could start questioning everyone in the room, I might actually make some headway. But I knew I couldn't just start questioning Tessa's customers without endangering her business even more. My gaze wandered from Patsy and her crew to the receptionist to the small, brave group of employees chasing down the runaway roaches. Even Tessa's employees might get nervous if they knew everything that was going on at the spa that day.

"Of course, everyone in town is probably going to know everything soon enough," I murmured as my gaze settled on Marletta, who was now holding a microphone to her face and speaking rapidly into the camera.

"Huh?" Bess glanced over at me.

I shot her an apologetic smile as I realized I'd spoken my thoughts loud enough for her to hear. "Nothing," I said. "I just realized there's one person here who might have seen something today who I haven't spoken to yet. Be right back."

Leaving a slightly confused-looking Bess behind, I dodged another roach and hurried toward Lulu. The young woman was standing just out of camera range, still holding the brush she'd used on her boss's hair as she watched Marletta at work.

"Hi," I said when I reached Lulu's side. I kept my voice quiet—I definitely didn't want my words picked up by the microphone. "You work for Marletta, right? My name's Nancy Drew."

Lulu glanced at me. "Hi," she said. "I'm Lulu. And yeah, I work for Marletta, for like six years now. I started with her right out of college. Why?"

I took a deep breath, trying to figure out how to

approach my question. "Um, you might have noticed that a few things have been going wrong at the spa today. Like this," I said, waving one hand toward the roach roundup. "I'm trying to help Tessa figure out who's behind it all. Since you guys have been here all day, I was just wondering if you've seen anything else that was weird or suspicious."

Lulu stared at me for a moment. Then she shrugged. "If there's anything going on, I'm sure Marletta will figure it out," she said. "She's the best investigative reporter I've ever known." She grimaced. "Even if the people at the station don't always remember that." Suddenly she let out a gasp. "Oh! That's probably it!"

"What?" I asked, my heart leaping. Had she just recalled some shady behavior she'd witnessed at the spa that day, some incriminating interview she'd heard?

"I bet it was one of the younger reporters at RH News," she said eagerly. "Like maybe that Stacey Kane. She's always trying to show up Marletta, make her look bad. She doesn't have a tenth of Marletta's experience, but just because she's young and pretty, she thinks she rules the place. Maybe she's trying to push Marletta out by sabotaging her story here or something, or . . ."

As she rambled on I swallowed a sigh, realizing

that Lulu wasn't looking like a very useful ally after all. But the assistant's crazy theory had put another idea in my head. What if Marletta herself had something to do with the sabotage? If she really was fearing for her job, as Lulu seemed to be saying, it might make the reporter desperate enough to try something a little sneaky. Maybe she was trying to drum up a good story for herself by causing trouble at the spa. Hadn't I just been thinking that this roach incident would probably make the lead story on that night's newscast?

And Marletta had certainly had the access necessary to pull all the pranks. She'd been wandering around the spa all day, mostly unaccompanied by anyone but her own people. It still seemed unlikely that such a well-known local journalist would risk her credibility and her reputation with such a silly stunt, but then again, it could be hard to predict what people might do if they were desperate enough. . . .

My eyes widened slightly as I noticed that even as Lulu continued to blab on and on about the evils of Stacey Kane, her fingers were busy cleaning a clump of blond hair out of the brush she was holding. My eyes widened as I noted how closely it resembled the clump I'd found in the kitchen earlier.

Of course, even if it was Marletta's hair, that didn't

necessarily mean she was guilty of planting that meat in the chili, or any of the other stuff. I had known all along that the hair might not even be a real clue, and I didn't want to put too much importance on it now.

"Lulu! Lipstick! Now!"

Lulu jumped as Marletta called to her. Glancing over, I saw that the cameraman was busy taping some close-up footage of the remaining roaches.

"Oops, gotta go," Lulu said to me, tucking the brush back into her shoulder bag and hurrying toward her boss.

I watched them for a moment, then turned away, feeling frustrated and impatient. The more I dug into this mystery, the more suspects I added to my list—and the less convinced I was that any of them really could have done it. I still had that nagging feeling from earlier, the feeling that there was some vital piece of the puzzle I was missing. If I could just figure out what that was, I had the feeling everything else would fall neatly into place.

Bess was still standing where I'd left her, but I noticed there was no sign of George. Noticing my expression, Bess rolled her eyes.

"She ran off again," she said. "Something about needing the bathroom. When I pointed out that she's spent half the day in the bathroom already, she just muttered something about indigestion from all the tofu and carrot juice and took off."

I sighed. George's disappearing act was getting really old. "Let's go outside for a sec," I suggested.

The hallway outside was deserted, though the noise of the crowd still drifted out there from the mud-bath room. Bess and I turned to face each other.

"Listen," she began. "This thing with George . . ."

I nodded. "It's gone on long enough, and it's getting a little annoying. I feel bad if she's sick or something, but I wish she'd just say so instead of taking off all the time. She's certainly not being her usual helpful self when it comes to this investigation—totally the opposite, in fact."

Bess's blue eyes looked worried. "I know," she said. "I think it's time to find her and make her tell us what's wrong."

"I agree," I said. "Let's split up and check the closest bathrooms. You go that way"—I pointed in the direction of the massage suite—"and I'll take the other direction. Let's meet back here."

We hurried off on our respective paths. The first bathroom I came to was completely empty. I tried to remember where the next one was located, and realized it was in the dining room. Spotting the door leading to the employees' hallway, I realized it would be faster to take a shortcut through the kitchen. It wasn't like anyone would complain. The entire kitchen staff was off ogling the bugs in the mud room.

I darted through the door and headed down the quiet hallway. I was so focused on my search for George, actually, that I barely slowed down as I reached the swinging doors into the kitchen—at least not until I nearly tripped over Lulu lying in the doorway!

12

Muddy Motives

I gasped, immediately falling to my knees at the young woman's side. "Lulu!" I cried, reaching for her. "Are you okay?"

Even before my fingers found the steady pulse in her neck, she groaned and stirred. Her dark eyes fluttered open, focusing blankly on me.

"Wha—what happened?" she croaked.

"I was just going to ask you the same thing," I said gently, helping her sit up. "How did you end up like this?"

Lulu put one hand to her forehead, looking groggy. "I—I was coming in here to get a glass of water for Marletta," she said slowly. She reached up to adjust her glasses, which had been knocked askew. "Someone grabbed me from behind. Then I felt something hit me on the head, and that's all I remember."

I nodded grimly. My gaze had just fallen on a stainless steel frying pan lying on the ground nearby. The bottom was dented outward, as if from a solid blow.

"Did you see the person who grabbed you?" I asked her. "Did he or she speak to you or anything?"

Lulu shook her head. "Not that I remember," she said, looking upset. She touched one hand to her frizzy dark hair. "It all happened so fast. . . ."

"That's okay," I assured her. "Just sit here for a minute. I'll get you a drink of water."

As I stood up I glanced at the frying pan again. I wondered if I should pick it up before the grease dripping out of it soaked into the carpet.

Then I smiled. A little lightbulb had just gone off in my head. I knew *exactly* who was behind all the sabotage at the spa!

Before I could do anything about it, I heard the sound of footsteps hurrying toward us. Glancing up, I saw Tessa rushing down the hall, followed by Marletta, Patsy, the chef, Bess, George, Deirdre, and at least half a dozen others.

"Oh, my goodness!" Tessa cried when she saw Lulu lying limply against the wall. "What happened here?"

I cleared my throat, ready to explain. But before I

could say a word, Marletta started shrieking. "Lulu!" she cried. "You poor dear! What happened to you?"

Lulu weakly repeated her story. Meanwhile Patsy bustled into the kitchen and returned with a glass of water. For the next minute or two there was a hubbub of activity as people gathered around Lulu, checked her for injuries, then carefully helped her into the dining room and seated her at a table.

Finally I saw my chance. Clearing my throat, I stepped to the center of the group, right in front of Lulu.

"Excuse me," I said loudly. "Could I have your attention, please? Tessa, I wanted to let you know that I finally uncovered who has been trying to sabotage your grand opening."

I waited as there was a sudden flurry of gasps and whispers from my gathered audience. I realized I was grandstanding a little, like a detective in a melodramatic old mystery movie, but I also knew it was probably necessary in this case. If I wanted to clear Tessa's reputation once and for all, I needed as many people as possible to witness what I was about to say next.

"What do you mean, Nancy?" Tessa asked, stepping forward with a note of cautious hope in her voice.

Noticing that Marletta's cameraman was taping, I answered her calmly. "I mean I know who put the meat in the chili earlier, and who fiddled with the controls of the steam room. I suspect this same person also sent an e-mail to Thomas Rackham, encouraging him in the protest that led to the lobby window being broken. And the very same person is the one who released those cockroaches in the mud room just now."

The room was completely silent. I had everyone's total attention. Even George seemed to have no interest in taking off for once.

"All this time, I'm been trying to figure out who had both the motive and the opportunity to pull all these disparate pranks," I continued. "Nobody was around when the meat was slipped into the chili— even Patsy had been called away on what turned out to be a false errand."

I glanced over at the chef. She was nodding at my words, looking curious.

"That means almost anyone could have planted the meat in the chili, whether a customer or an employee or even someone off the street," I went on. "The steam room is sort of the same thing. The controls are outside, so with the door closed, the victim would never notice someone messing with them."

This time I glanced at Deirdre. She was frowning slightly, probably remembering her own bright-red face.

"And then there was the rock-throwing incident," I said. "Of course, we know who did that. There were plenty of witnesses, and besides, Thomas confessed."

"Are you saying that Thomas was behind all the sabotage?" Deirdre asked skeptically. "No way, Nancy! Even if he could have sneaked away from the protest long enough to do the meat thing and the sauna thing, he couldn't possibly have released those roaches. He was already at the police station by the time that happened!"

I nodded. "Exactly," I said.

"So are you saying Thomas had a partner in crime?" Bess guessed. "Someone on the inside who was working with him or something?"

"Nope." I shook my head. "I don't think Thomas had anything to do with the other pranks at all. In fact, I think the person who sent him that e-mail, and did everything else, is right here in this room!"

There was an audible gasp. I almost smiled at the melodrama of it all, but I forced myself to remain straight faced as I glanced around at my audience. They were staring at me with amazement, confusion, and curiosity—except for one person, whose expression had suddenly gone nervous and shifty eyed.

That was enough to confirm it for me. I continued on, wanting to get it over with now that I knew my hunch was correct.

I pointed to the frying pan lying beneath the swinging doors. "That's what gave me the answer I needed," I announced. "Lulu said someone hit her from behind, and the dented frying pan was the obvious weapon. But I noticed that the pan had been used recently. In fact, it's still dripping with oil!"

"Olive oil," Patsy put in helpfully.

"Right," I said. "But as you'll all notice, Lulu's hair is perfectly dry." I pointed to the assistant, who was cowering on her stool, looking terrified. "If she'd really been knocked out with the bottom of that pan, her whole head would be dripping with oil right now!"

I was ready to continue with the rest of my evidence, but it wasn't necessary. At that moment Lulu let out a wild shriek, leaped to her feet, and made a break for the door.

She only made it a few yards before someone grabbed her. After a brief struggle she suddenly went limp and started sobbing uncontrollably.

"I'm so sorry, Marletta," Lulu wailed through her tears. "I did it for you! I thought it would help. . . . I didn't know they would figure it out. . . ."

I winced, hearing the real pain in her voice. As happy as I was to see the mystery solved, I couldn't help feeling a little sorry for Lulu. I glanced behind me to see my friends' reactions.

They were both staring at Lulu with a combination of pity and relief on their faces. Meanwhile I noticed that Patsy had taken a few steps toward them and was peering curiously at George.

"George?" the chef said in surprise, a split second before George bolted for the door yet again. "George Fayne? Is that you?"

A little while later I shifted my weight, sighing with pleasure as I felt warm, soft mud squish between my toes. Once the giant cockroaches had been removed, the mud bath turned out to be every bit as luxurious as promised. And, since a few of the other patrons seemed reluctant to give it a try so soon after the bug incident, my friends and I had one large tub all to ourselves. I just hoped that it wouldn't take long for everyone to realize what they were missing.

"This place is totally awesome," Bess said lazily, as if reading my mind.

"Yeah, yeah." George sounded less relaxed, and more impatient. "Mud, schmud. I'm still waiting for Nancy to fill us in on how she figured out Lulu was behind everything."

Even though nearly an hour had passed since the sobbing Lulu had been dragged off by the police, my friends still hadn't heard all the details of the case. Things at the spa had been pretty busy since Lulu's confession, and I'd been surrounded for a while—first by Marletta, who wanted to get the whole thing on tape, and then by a grateful Tessa and dozens of curious customers. I'd only had a few moments to talk with Lulu herself, though I'd managed to turn up a few more puzzle pieces in that brief conversation. Lulu seemed so eager not to incriminate her boss by her own actions that she'd blurted out all sorts of interesting information before Chief McGinnis had handcuffed her and taken her away.

"Well, I already told you how I noticed the oil on the frying pan," I said. "The shape of the dent indicated that the blow came on the inside of the pan. But that would have left an oily spot on Lulu's head, and—"

"Right," George interrupted. "We know that already. But even with all that, how did you know she was behind the other stuff too?"

Bess nodded. "She could have staged her own attack for unrelated reasons," she pointed out. "Like trying to create a story for her boss to cover, for instance."

"Well," I said, sinking a little lower in the bath until the mud almost touched my chin, "it was sort of a process-of-elimination thing. See, I'd just been thinking over who might have had the opportunity to commit all the sabotage. It even occurred to me that Marletta herself had plenty of access to the spa all day. That meant Lulu had the same access—maybe even more, since she wasn't as noticeable as Marletta."

"That's true," George said, flicking a spot of mud off her shoulder. "But why? What was she trying to accomplish?"

"That's what really cracked the case for me," I replied. "When I figured out her motive. Didn't you guys notice how devoted Lulu seemed to be to Marletta?"

"I did," Bess said. "She practically idolized her."

I nodded. "That's why she was so desperate to help her when she thought she was in trouble," I explained. "See, when I questioned Lulu about whether she'd seen anything suspicious at the spa today, she started off on some tangent about how the younger reporters at the TV station are all out to get Marletta." I shrugged. "I guess that part may have some truth to it—Marletta is quite a bit older than most of the others, and that can't be easy in the TV business."

"True," Bess said thoughtfully, sticking one toe up out of the mud and staring at it. "It's too bad, really. But I guess it's not surprising if Lulu was worried about Marletta's career."

"Especially if she kept getting stuck with minor

pieces like covering the grand opening of a new spa," George pointed out.

"Right," I said. "Actually, I suspect Marletta *wanted* to cover this story because of the whole vegetarian angle. But Lulu must have freaked out when she heard her boss was doing what could be considered a fluff piece, instead of the hard news stories she's known for. She must have thought it was a sign Marletta was being eased out."

Understanding dawned on George's face. "And so Lulu figured a big, scandalous scoop would be just the thing to get her boss front and center again—keep her job safe for a while longer."

"Exactly," I said. "And I guess she didn't want to take any chances. Not only did she send that anonymous e-mail to Thomas, hoping to stir up trouble that way, but she also smuggled in the meat and put it in the chili. Oh, and she also must have dropped that clump of Marletta's hair while she was in the kitchen. Anyway, she knew the chili thing would definitely get Marletta all riled up."

"But then you stumbled on it before she could get Marletta to the kitchen to 'discover' it, and her plan was ruined," Bess said with a smile.

"Uh-huh." I sifted some mud through my hand, thinking about how lucky that had been. If I hadn't been looking for George right at that moment . . .

That reminded me that Bess and I still didn't know what had been making her act so strangely all day. I suspected it might have something to do with Patsy recognizing her earlier, but I wasn't sure how, since George had disappeared for a while after that, and I hadn't had a chance to ask her about it since she'd turned up again. Maybe it was finally time.

Before I could say anything, Bess spoke again. "So the turtle demonstration thing worked, but the cops broke it up before Marletta could get much footage," she remembered. "Then the chili thing fizzled, thanks to you. She must have freaked out at that point."

"Yep." I smiled. Bess was always good at seeing other people's emotions and motives once she had all the information. "That's when she started trying things on impulse—pretty much whatever she could do without being caught, including the sauna thing." I grinned. "She told me she saw Deirdre go in and chose her steam room purposely, figuring she'd be sure to make a major stink."

My friends laughed. "Well, she got that part right," George commented.

"She said she did a bunch of other stuff too," I went on. "Stuff that no one even noticed, like tampering with the massage oil and switching ingredients in the facial lab and things like that. In fact, she was so busy with that stuff that she was late in noticing the window-breaking thing. She blamed herself for Marletta being late on the scene that time."

"But that's silly," Bess said. "She couldn't know that he was going to do that."

I shrugged. "I know, but I guess she was panicking by then," I said. "That's when she realized she needed something big and dramatic if her plan was going to work, so she hit upon sabotaging the mud bath. She'd noticed the pet store earlier, when some of the protestors headed over there, and she must've known about Bug Alley. When the others went back inside, she ducked out just long enough to run across the street. She told me she was planning to release some worms or crickets in the mud, but when she saw those Madagascar hissing cockroaches, she knew they'd be even better. She was able to release them through one of the vents, and finally her plan seemed to be working."

"That's for sure," Bess said with a slight shudder.

"Then I approached her in the mud room, and she started to panic again," I continued. "I was really just asking her for her input since I thought she might have seen something. But I guess she knew who I was, and thought maybe I was getting suspicious of her or something."

My friends exchanged a grin. "Imagine that,"

George said. "Getting nervous when Nancy Drew starts questioning you. Go figure."

I could feel my face blush. "Anyway, she decided to clear herself by making herself into a victim," I said. "Even though practically everyone was in the mud room at the time, I guess she figured her 'attack' might make everyone think someone from the outside was responsible for the sabotage. That way she'd be in the clear, and Marletta would still get her story."

"Well, part of her plan worked, didn't it?" Bess pointed out. "Marletta did get a heck of a story. She and her cameraman were taping away the whole time the police were dragging Lulu off to jail. Talk about drama!"

I sighed. "I know," I said. "That one will make the lead story tonight for sure. I have to admit, I can't help feeling a little sorry for Lulu, though."

"I know what you mean," Bess agreed. "Even though her actions were wrong, and she could have ruined Tessa's business, her motive was really sort of sweet. . . ."

"Speaking of motives," I said, suddenly remembering the last remaining unresolved mystery, "there's one more bit of weird behavior I'd really like to hear an explanation for."

Bess nodded. "Me too."

We both turned to gaze inquisitively at George. For a second she pretended not to know what was going on. But the force of our stares wore her down quickly, and she broke into a sheepish grin.

"Okay, okay," she said. "I guess you'll probably figure it out soon anyway, now that Patsy spotted me." She took a deep breath. "It just so happens that I'm broke right now."

Bess and I laughed. "So what else is new?" Bess quipped.

George snorted. "Go ahead and laugh," she said. "But this is serious. My last modem is about to croak, and if I don't get some cash soon to buy a new one I'll be totally cut off from the Internet for who knows how long."

That made us laugh again. George is as attached to her Internet connection as Bess is to her blow dryer and makeup brushes.

"Anyway, Mom refused to give me another advance on my catering paycheck, so I needed to figure out another way to earn some quick cash," George said. Now that she was confessing at last, she seemed almost relieved, her words tumbling out one after another. "So I applied for a bunch of part-time jobs, including one right here at the spa, scrubbing vegetables in the kitchen." She shrugged. "I never heard back from them, so I figured I didn't get the job. That's why I wasn't exactly thrilled about coming here. And I especially didn't want to run into Patsy or the other kitchen people I met during my interview."

"Ah!" I exclaimed as the last puzzle piece fell into place. That explained why George had been skittering around like a nervous cat all day—and also why she hadn't told us about it. She has a stubborn streak of pride that gets in her way sometimes.

Bess nodded as she, too, finally understood. "I'm sorry you didn't get the job," she told George.

George shrugged. "That's the thing," she said. "I just found out from Patsy that I *did* get it. I'd told her to e-mail me, but I guess my last stupid modem messed up again and I never got the message. So they hired someone else!"

"That's too bad," I said sympathetically. "But don't worry. Maybe Bess and I can help you figure something out."

Just then one of the mud room doors flew open. Glancing up, I saw Deirdre hurry into the room, followed by Tessa. Deirdre had changed out of her Indulgences robe and slippers, back into her street clothes.

"Nancy!" Deirdre cried, her voice more cheerful than I'd ever heard it. "Great news! Tessa just told me she wants to give us a reward for solving the mystery!"

"Us?" I repeated. "You mean you and me?"

"Right," Deirdre said with a touch of impatience. "I just explained to her how we worked together and everything, and she wants to give us a three-hundred-dollar reward—that's one-fifty for each of us."

For a moment I was stunned that Deirdre was claiming half the credit for solving the case. But I shook that off quickly. Knowing Deirdre, it really wasn't surprising at all.

"It's the least I can do," Tessa spoke up with a smile. "You girls really saved the day. It's still going to take some work to make people forget about that roach incident, but at least now everyone will know the culprit has been caught. I owe you girls my business. Thank you so much!"

"You're welcome," I told her. "But I don't need your money. I was happy to help."

"Don't be stupid, Nancy," Deirdre said before Tessa could answer. "I'm sure it will make Tessa feel good to repay us, even in this little way." She smiled broadly at the spa owner. "We'd be happy to accept the reward."

"Fine," I said calmly. "Thanks, Tessa. But if you insist on a reward, I really think we'd better split it four ways. Deirdre was a big help, of course"—I shot her a sugary smile—"but we never could have solved this case without Bess and George." I gestured toward my friends. "So we'll just split that reward four ways if that's okay with you."

"Of course!" Tessa said. She glanced at her watch. "Now if you'll excuse me . . ." With one last smile and thank-you, she hurried out of the room.

"Wow!" George said. "Thanks, Nancy. That was cool of you. Looks like I'll be able to get that new modem sooner than I thought!"

"Good," I said. "And you're totally welcome."

When I looked over at Deirdre again, she was scowling. "What's the big idea splitting the reward with *them*?" she demanded, stepping closer to the tub, her hands on her hips. "I wouldn't have gone to all that trouble and messed up my own day at the spa for a measly seventy-five bucks!"

"You're lucky you're getting anything at all," George shot back. "It's not like you really helped out all that much. Nancy was the one who figured it out—you had nothing to do with it."

"It's okay, George," I said quickly, hoping to soothe them both before we had a real fight on our hands. "Deirdre actually did help out a lot. She earned her share of the reward."

"That's right," Bess spoke up, obviously sharing my thoughts about the other two girls. "It's no big deal. Let's not ruin this nice, relaxing mud bath with an argument, okay?"

Despite our best efforts, I was fully expecting George to continue sniping at Deirdre. To my surprise, though, George's angry face broke into a smile.

"You know, you're right, Bess," she said. "You too, Nancy. DeeDee—um, I mean, Deirdre—I'm sorry. Truce?" She held out a hand toward the other girl.

Deirdre looked slightly suspicious. "Well, I still don't think you and Bess really earned *any* reward," she muttered half under her breath. But she stepped toward George. "Still, I suppose I can be the bigger person about this." She took George's outstretched hand.

George grasped it and shook it. "Good," she said. "And I want to show you exactly how much we appreciate all you've done. . . ."

At that she gave a sudden hard yank. Deirdre let out a startled yip as she lost her balance and fell forward—right into the mud bath!

The next few seconds were a flurry of laughter (from George), quick escapes (Bess and me), and shrieks (Deirdre, of course). Soon Bess and I found ourselves on the far side of the mud pool, watching as the fully-clothed Deirdre yelled angrily at a hysterically laughing George.

"I bet that's the last time for a while that Deirdre is likely to help us out with one of your mysteries, Nancy," Bess said with a laugh as we backed farther away from the sputtering, mud-covered Deirdre.

I grinned, wiping mud spatters off my face with the back of one hand. "You might be right," I told her. "But the civility was sort of nice while it lasted!"

REDISCOVER THE CLASSIC MYSTERIES OF NANCY DREW

$5.99 ($8.99 CAN) each
AVAILABLE AT YOUR LOCAL BOOKSTORE OR LIBRARY

Grosset & Dunlap • A division of Penguin Young Readers Group
A member of Penguin Group (USA), Inc. • A Pearson Company
www.penguin.com/youngreaders

star power

by Catherine Hapka

She's beautiful, she's talented, she's famous.

She's a star!

Things would be perfect
if only her family
was around to help
her celebrate. . . .

Follow the
adventures of
fourteen-year-old
pop star
Star Calloway

HAVE YOU READ ALL OF THE ALICE BOOKS?

PHYLLIS REYNOLDS NAYLOR

STARTING WITH ALICE
Atheneum Books for
  Young Readers
  0-689-84395-X
Aladdin Paperbacks
  0-689-84396-8

ALICE IN BLUNDERLAND
Atheneum Books for
  Young Readers
  0-689-84397-6
Aladdin Paperbacks
  0-689-84398-4

LOVINGLY ALICE
Atheneum Books for
  Young Readers
  0-689-84399-2
Aladdin Paperbacks
  0-689-84400-X

THE AGONY OF ALICE
Atheneum Books for
  Young Readers
  0-689-31143-5
Aladdin Paperbacks
  0-689-81672-3

ALICE IN RAPTURE,
  SORT-OF
Atheneum Books for
  Young Readers
  0-689-31466-3
Aladdin Paperbacks
  0-689-81687-1

RELUCTANTLY ALICE
Atheneum Books for
  Young Readers
  0-689-31681-X
Aladdin Paperbacks
  0-689-81688-X

ALL BUT ALICE
Atheneum Books for
  Young Readers
  0-689-31773-5
Aladdin Paperbacks
  0-689-85044-1

ALICE IN APRIL
Atheneum Books for
  Young Readers
  0-689-31805-7
Aladdin Paperbacks
  0-689-81686-3

ALICE IN-BETWEEN
Atheneum Books for
  Young Readers
  0-689-31890-0
Aladdin Paperbacks
  0-689-81685-5

ALICE THE BRAVE
Atheneum Books for
  Young Readers
  0-689-80095-9
Aladdin Paperbacks
  0-689-80598-5

ALICE IN LACE
Atheneum Books for
  Young Readers
  0-689-80358-3
Aladdin Paperbacks
  0-689-80597-7

OUTRAGEOUSLY ALICE
Atheneum Books for
  Young Readers
  0-689-80354-0
Aladdin Paperbacks
  0-689-80596-9

ACHINGLY ALICE
Atheneum Books for
  Young Readers
  0-689-80533-9
Aladdin Paperbacks
  0-689-80595-0
Simon Pulse
  0-689-86396-9

ALICE ON THE OUTSIDE
Atheneum Books for
  Young Readers
  0-689-80359-1
Simon Pulse
  0-689-80594-2

GROOMING OF ALICE
Atheneum Books for
  Young Readers
  0-689-82633-8
Simon Pulse
  0-689-84618-5

ALICE ALONE
Atheneum Books for
  Young Readers
  0-689-82634-6
Simon Pulse
  0-689-85189-8

SIMPLY ALICE
Atheneum Books for
  Young Readers
  0-689-84751-3
Simon Pulse
  0-689-85965-1

PATIENTLY ALICE
Atheneum Books for
  Young Readers
  0-689-82636-2
Simon Pulse
  0-689-87073-6

INCLUDING ALICE
Atheneum Books for
  Young Readers
  0-689-82637-0
Simon Pulse
  0-689-87074-4

ALICE ON HER WAY
Atheneum Books for
  Young Readers
  0-689-87090-6